"I won't keep you long," he said

"It isn't a lengthy process, I understand."

Barbara stared at the Marques Ruy Nieves dos Santos, trying to quell her forboding. "What isn't?"

"Proposing marriage." At Barbara's audible gasp, he murmured, "You were expecting something different?"

He knew quite well what she'd been expecting, Barbara thought, coloring furiously. Moreover, after that terrible night, she had every justification for expecting it. She drew a deep breath.

"Don't be unkind," he said reproachfully. "You're very intimidating."

Barbara snorted and shook her head in confusion. It had never occurred to her that he might want to marry her. Of course, she corrected herself, he didn't *want* to marry her. But it was extraordinary that he would think her suitable even for an alliance of convenience like this.

SOPHIE WESTON wrote and illustrated her first book at
the age of five. After university she decided on a career in
international finance, which was tremendously
stimulating and demanding, but it was not enough.
Something was missing in her life, and that something
turned out to be writing. These days her life is complete.
She loves exciting travel and adventures, yet hates to
stray too long from her homey cottage in Chelsea, where
she writes.

Books by Sophie Weston

HARLEQUIN PRESENTS

838—EXECUTIVE LADY
870—A STRANGER'S TOUCH
918—LIKE ENEMIES
942—SHADOW PRINCESS
957—YESTERDAY'S MIRROR
980—BEYOND RANSOM
1014—CHALLENGE

HARLEQUIN ROMANCE

1925—BEWARE THE HUNTSMAN
2005—GOBLIN COURT
2129—WIFE TO CHARLES
2218—UNEXPECTED HAZARD
2362—AN UNDEFENDED CITY

Don't miss any of our special offers. Write to us at the
following address for information on our newest releases.

Harlequin Reader Service
901 Fuhrmann Blvd., P.O. Box 1397, Buffalo, NY 14240
Canadian address: P.O. Box 603,
Fort Erie, Ont. L2A 5X3

SOPHIE WESTON

a matter of feeling

Harlequin Books

TORONTO • NEW YORK • LONDON
AMSTERDAM • PARIS • SYDNEY • HAMBURG
STOCKHOLM • ATHENS • TOKYO • MILAN

Harlequin Presents first edition February 1990
ISBN 0-373-11246-7

Original hardcover edition published in 1989
by Mills & Boon Limited

CHAPTER ONE

IT WAS odd, Barbara thought afterwards, but it started out as an ordinary day. She had no sense of impending disaster when she got up. She dressed, brushed her chestnut hair until it gleamed in the mirror, and ran downstairs and out into the street as cheerfully as if her whole life was not about to be thrown back into the melting-pot. The only niggling unpleasantness at the back of her mind was the knowledge that sooner or later she would have to speak to Trevor Bowman about the deal he was running behind her back. She even sang as she walked briskly to the Tube station; it was that sort of morning.

As usual, she was there before anyone else. She liked to be. It meant that she could sort out the major queries before Trevor breezed in and set the whole office in an uproar. Trevor was young, dynamic and very successful, but he was no organiser. That was why he had recruited Barbara as a junior partner when he had first set up his estate agency. Barbara not only knew a great deal about property, she could run a busy office single-handed, if necessary, while he and Dan Leonard got on with the legwork.

Barbara smiled rather ruefully as she rifled swiftly through the day's post. She could run the office, all right, but only if she had some time to herself, away from Trevor's whirlwind activities.

For the first months of their partnership she had had very little of that. He had included her in everything, at first wanting to impress her, then rather sulkily, as if he resented her increasing success with their Spanish and Portuguese clients. Her fluency in Spanish and Portuguese was greater than his, so it had seemed quite natural to Barbara that those clients should ask for her by name. But Trevor hadn't liked it. Not a bit.

When she realised that he was doing business behind her back with someone she would normally have expected to meet, she had assumed at first that it was a show of professional jealousy, Trevor's determination to prove that he could handle a Spanish-speaking client without assistance from Barbara Lamb. But she had the uneasy feeling that his secrecy meant more than that; and she knew the signs, for heaven's sake, of someone conducting a shady business deal. The casualness that didn't quite work, the air of suppressed excitement...

She had recognised them in her Uncle Harry when she'd last seen him, and had known in that moment that she was going to have to confront Trevor and demand to know what he had been up to. Even if his undercover deal wasn't actually illegal, if he got into hot water, she and Dan would be dragged with him. That was the point of a partnership. One partner was responsible for the others: debts, business, ethics... Barbara shivered, and got on with the post.

There was a letter with a Puerto Banus postmark, and she set it on one side to deal with at once. There were a number of others from abroad, none that she judged urgent. She left them for Rosemary, Trevor's and her secretary, to open. Then her fingers paused among the pile of envelopes. A handwritten envelope was in itself a rarity, and this handwriting was one she felt she knew. She hesitated, then flipped the letter over. Sometimes correspondents put their addresses on the back. But no, not in this case.

She dropped it, shrugging. Probably a new client. Rosemary would deal with it and refer whoever it was to the right person. Rosemary, though young and still in her first job, was a joy of efficiency.

The outer door banged. Barbara looked up as the new arrival came through into the small office behind the open-plan reception area.

''Morning,' said Dan Leonard cheerfully. 'Lovely day. Napoleon not in yet?'

Trevor was not popular with his staff, but only Dan, who was as good a salesman and a better-informed property expert, made it obvious. Barbara bit her lip. 'He said something last night about picking up an important client from the airport. He said he'd probably be in late.'

Dan showed no sign of surprise, only saying drily, 'Fair enough. He didn't ask you to go along?'

She shook her head. 'No, but I'm glad he didn't. I prefer to start the day with a clear in-tray.'

'When do you ever do anything else, Barbara, my sweet? You're wasted nursing Trevor, you know.'

She didn't answer. Dan was the only person who would say that, too, though she was vaguely aware that the opinion was shared by most of the seven people who worked for Trevor.

She put the unopened letters on Rosemary's desk and went back to her own. Dan watched her ironically, almost clinically. There was no offence in it. She had known him as long as she had known Trevor, and none of them had ever felt any attraction to each other. That was one of the reasons she had agreed to join them when they first set up their own agency. Attraction made Barbara feel uncomfortable, and with Dan and Trevor she had never had to endure that discomfort. At least...

She knew that what Dan could see was a slight girl, above medium height, quietly dressed in a dark navy suit and a crisp blouse with a deep collar and a thin bootlace tie. She had good bones too, and her fashionably cropped hair gleamed the colour of new-minted sovereigns, somewhere between chestnut and gold. She had a perfect skin, like a child's, and the lashes that so often veiled hidden laughter in her hazel eyes were as long and curling as any professional beauty might wish. She had no idea that Dan was thinking that efficient Barbara Lamb could have been stunning if she chose. His keen eye had long ago discerned that she had more spirit than she usually allowed to show, and he was wondering, not for the first time, why she chose to look so unobtrusive. Surely most women wanted to enhance their looks rather than hide them? He busied himself making coffee, and soon the bubbling liquid began to give off an inviting aroma.

Barbara looked up from her work, her nose twitching.

'How long?' she asked with a laugh.

'Five minutes,' he said with the assurance of long practice. 'Time to get that lot out of the way before you have the first cup of the day.'

Barbara laughed, and went back to her correspondence. She had scribbled a draft reply to one letter, confirmed a series of estimates in response to another and dictated a telex to Spain to answer a question posed by a third, before she looked up to find Dan pouring coffee into the mug on her desk. By now Rosemary had appeared, windblown and smiling, and had taken her seat in the outer office to deal with customers, deftly slipping the inevitable bag of crisps into her desk drawer.

'That child,' Dan commented, 'eats more junk food than anyone else I know. In fact, she eats more than anyone I know, period. And she's as thin as a rake.'

'It's not fair,' Barbara agreed, amused, tipping her chair back to sip the warm, fragrant liquid. Dan stared at her.

'You don't need to envy Rosemary. I'd say you were too thin, if anything. Are you losing weight, Barbara?'

She was. It wasn't that she felt ill, but ever since that last time Harry had descended on her it had been so much easier to skip the occasional meal. It meant that she didn't have to wear laddered tights, could afford to have her shoes repaired and her hair trimmed as regularly as ever, that she could pay her rent on time... The waistbands of her suits had begun to loosen, and her blouses seemed baggier than they had ever been, but she was surprised that anyone else had noticed. She shrugged.

Dan said softly, 'Something on your mind?'

Barbara buried her nose in her coffee-mug. Dan sat down in the chair opposite her and leaned his elbows on her desk.

'Don't let Napoleon get you down,' he said with a shrewdness that surprised her.

Her eyes flew to his face. When she was startled or alarmed they had a habit of going very wide and blank, like a cat's.

'I know Trevor, too,' Dan reminded her. 'I don't like some of the deals he's getting into now. And nor do you, do you? That's why he's keeping them to himself. He's had some damned odd characters coming to see him. Especially late in the evening.'

Barbara sighed. It was worrying to have her worst fears voiced so cogently as this. For weeks now she had been clinging to the hope that they were mistaken.

She said, 'Have you met any of them? He won't let me see them.'

Dan nodded slowly. 'Nor me. It was by chance.' He grinned. 'Well, almost. I'd left my raincoat behind, so I came back, and he had this Spanish chap here. They were talking about some development along the coast, from Spain right up to the Algarve. It sounded like mega-bucks to me.'

'That doesn't mean it's crooked,' objected Barbara.

Dan gave her a pitying look. 'It does if a million-aire developer comes to a three-partner agency like ours when he could go to any one of the international agencies and get a hundred times the contacts.'

Barbara said, 'But we've got very good contacts in Spain and Portugal.'

'*You* have,' Dan pointed out softly. 'You're the one who can talk to them on their own terms. Trevor just fleeces the Brits. But you're our selling point on Spanish property. And he won't let you get near the deal, will he?' He shrugged. 'Q.E.D.'

He stood up. 'Well, I'll get on with my work. You,' he leaned forward and flicked her completed pile, 'shame me.'

He left Barbara deep in thought. It seemed that she was haunted by dubious characters, she thought with a flicker of irritation that bordered on pain. Not only was there Harry, reminding her every time he turned up that she came from a family of cheats and confidence tricksters and still had her debts to pay. Now there was Trevor, getting deeply involved in something she did not understand and so mistrusted. She *must* talk to Trevor, she thought. Dan wouldn't. Of them all, he had the most to lose, with his mortgage and his young family dependent on him for every penny. But she had no one dependent on her. And she could challenge Trevor.

She pushed her hand through her soft, gleaming hair, her eyes clouding. Though she would rather not: *how* she would rather not!

Trevor came in an hour and a half later, suspiciously pleased with himself. The important client—whom he carefully didn't name—had been left at his hotel. Trevor whirled in, kissed Barbara enthusiastically on both cheeks, and then retired behind a number of glossy brochures showing golf courses and swimming pools.

Barbara drew a deep breath. This was it, she thought: ask him. Ask him what he's up to. But as she rose to her feet she heard a sound from the doorway, and turned, half annoyed and half relieved.

Rosemary stood in the doorway, looking put out.

'There's a woman to see you,' she said. 'No appointment, but she said you'd see her.' She looked at the piece of scrap paper in her hand and spelt out laboriously, 'Pepita Martinez.' She looked up, half embarrassed, and defiant. 'She said you knew her.'

Barbara started to speak, but Trevor came over and interrupted, frowning. 'Martinez? I don't think... What's she like?'

Rosemary sniffed. 'About thirty. *Wonderful* clothes, black hair like a ballet dancer. Good English.'

Maybe it was the latter that swayed Trevor. Normally he did not see clients who walked in off the street. He said, 'OK, send her in.'

But when Miss Martinez came in it was Barbara who moved forward in spontaneous pleasure.

'Pepita!'

The Spanish girl embraced her warmly, exclaiming in her own language. Trevor's face clouded. He said nastily, 'Do I take it this is a social visit, Senhorinha Martinez?'

Pepita disengaged herself from Barbara and turned to look at him coolly.

'I hoped for a word with Barbara, certainly,' she said in a voice whose charming accent did not disguise the fact that she found Trevor less than impressive. 'I thought perhaps we might talk—privately.'

Trevor said with firmness, 'I'm afraid that's impossible unless it's about business. We're very pressed at the moment, Senhorinha Martinez.'

Pepita looked at him limpidly. 'Oh, it is definitely about business.'

'Then I will be delighted to talk to you,' he said, gesturing at the chair in front of his desk.

She shook her head quite gently. 'Barbara,' she said with a firmness that echoed his own.

Trevor's face began to darken again.

Barbara said hastily, 'Why don't we go somewhere for a cup of coffee? Then we can leave Trevor undisturbed. And I can report back,' she added placatingly.

She was going to have to have a good story when she returned to the office, she realised. She said as much to Pepita when they seated themselves in the lounge of the fashionable hotel at which Pepita was staying and to which she had insisted on returning. Pepita gave a grin, very reminiscent of the girl she had been, and quite at variance with the elegance of her new clothes.

'Yes, he looked as if he could be a nuisance,' she said tranquilly. 'What is he to you?'

Barbara stared. Pepita had always been alarmingly frank about personal matters, but this was rapid, even for her. They had not met for five years, after all, and in the taxi coming here had exchanged nothing more than pleasantries.

'I hope he is not your lover,' Pepita went on, still in that calm tone. 'He was rude and he looked stupid.'

Barbara swallowed, tried to feel indignant, and in the end laughed. 'You're incorrigible,' she said.

'You mean he is?' Pepita's strong dark brows met across her creamy forehead.

'No. Trevor and I are colleagues and nothing more.'

'Oh.' Pepita digested this, still frowning a little. 'He seemed very—possessive?' she said in a faint note of query.

'About his job. He normally deals with clients face to face, not me.'

'I see.' Pepita looked relieved but thoughtful. 'So is there someone else?'

Barbara shook her head. 'Pepita, we knew each other ten years ago. Since then we've met once, for a couple of days. We haven't done more than exchange Christmas cards for three years, then suddenly you turn up and grill me about my love-life. Why?'

Pepita bit her lip. Then she said, 'I suppose that's the way my mind is running at the moment.' Her voice sounded stifled. And then her eyes lifted to Barbara's. 'You obviously haven't heard.'

Barbara shook her head, bewildered.

'I'm engaged,' Pepita said bluntly. 'To Ruy Nieves dos Santos.'

The bottom fell out of Barbara's stomach. She stared at her friend blindly, as if she was not there;

as if the muted bustle of the lounge, the attentive waiters and the soft music did not exist. She had never wanted to hear that name again. And now Pepita, once her best friend, was saying she was going to marry him.

'And I wish I wasn't,' said Pepita, sending the world further into tumbling chaos. 'I don't know why I said I would. He scares me.'

Barbara stared at her, numb. Her mind could form no words at all.

Pepita leaned forward urgently. 'I need your help, Barbara—really. Please! I—don't know what to do.'

Taking Barbara's silence for consent—or at least for sympathy—Pepita plunged into an account of her betrothal. Ruy Nieves dos Santos had first proposed, it seemed, over a year ago.

'At first I couldn't face it,' she said frankly. 'He's too—well, you know what he's like.'

'Yes,' said Barbara, through lips that felt as if they had been anaesthetised.

'He's so—remote. I've known him for years and he can still frighten me.' Pepita looked slightly ashamed.

Barbara said again numbly, 'Yes.'

'Mama was delighted, of course. You can imagine.'

Barbara thought back to the cosy, cheerful Senhora Martinez, a widow of some years who had left her native Spain to set up home on the southern Portuguese coast. When Barbara knew them, Pepita had been keeping the ramshackle household going by running a small riding school and writing a number of crisp letters to her mother's sleepy and increasingly nervous trustees. Notwithstanding Pepita's efficiency, Barbara could well imagine that the Senhora would greet her impending marriage to a wealthy man with tears of joy.

'She started pushing me,' said Pepita. 'I didn't realise it at the time. It was all terribly subtle: First of all it was, "If you and Ruy were to marry, I wouldn't worry about you any more." Then it was, "When you get married..." Then she started talking about grandchildren!' She looked at Barbara in despair. 'Grandchildren, I ask you!' She lifted her shoulders. 'I couldn't take any more. I gave in.' She looked at Barbara under her lashes with unwarranted intentness. 'I shouldn't have done. I can't face it.'

Barbara said, 'Is that why you're in London? Running away?'

'No, I'm supposed to be here buying clothes for the wedding. Ruy's here, too. His grandmother is in a clinic. He's talking to the doctors.'

'Wedding?' Barbara felt slightly sick, though she did not know why. It was nothing to her, after all, that Pepita was marrying the Marquês Nieves dos Santos, except that she might have wished her friend a happier fate.

'It's supposed to be quiet because of the Marquesa's health. Next month, Ruy said.' Suddenly Pepita gave a shiver and her hands clasped tightly together in her lap.

Barbara's eyes were drawn irresistibly to her long-fingered hands. She wore rings on every finger, just as she used to ten years ago, but they were cheap dress rings. There was no heavy betrothal diamond there.

Pepita allowed the waiter to fuss with the coffee-pot and a silver jug of cream, to pass a dish of sugared pastries, then waved him away.

'It was when I started to think about it . . . just another four weeks of being my own woman . . . I couldn't do it.'

There was no mistaking the note of desperation in her voice.

Barbara said, 'What did the Marquês say when you told him?'

She did not want to know. She quite desperately did not want to know how Ruy Nieves dos Santos took being jilted. But she could not help herself: she had to ask.

Pepita stirred her coffee with concentration. 'Ah—yes. That's the problem.'

'Is he going to sue you for breach of promise?'

Pepita did not look up. 'Probably,' she said in an absent voice. Then with great decision, she put down the coffee-cup and swung round on the velvet-covered couch to face Barbara directly. She looked apprehensive and determined.

'I haven't told him. I don't know how to. And Mama—she'll collapse. I told you, I need help.'

Barbara straightened against the luxurious cushions. 'You can't mean . . .' she said slowly.

But Pepita was nodding. 'Ruy knows you. You're the only person in London I can ask. I'd ask the Marquesa, but she's so ill. And I can't face him—you know what he's like. He'll think it's because of his scar.'

Barbara had gone cold. 'Why?'

'Oh, he always does.' Pepita was almost bab-bling in her desire to persuade her friend. 'He won't talk about it, he's too proud. But he always sits so that side of his face is in darkness. Haven't you noticed? And the stupid woman that Fernando married called him a monster and said she didn't want him in any of the wedding photographs. Ruy said to me once that I'd have a wedding album out of the Chamber of Horrors, and did I mind that?'

'And did you?' said Barbara blankly, trying to get hold of some sense of reality in this crazy situ-ation of Pepita's.

Pepita hesitated, and gave her an oddly calcu-lating look. 'I'm not sure. I didn't think so. But when it got closer to being married, and he started to——' She shivered again.

Barbara stared. Pepita was a practical girl, and a riding stable was a place where the earthier side of life was inescapable. It was not like her to be embarrassed about facts.

'You mean when he started to make love to you?'

Pepita was shocked. 'Of course not! That's the sort of thing he does with his girlfriends, the women who don't matter. He wouldn't make love to his future wife until we're married. He'd think it was insulting.'

'Oh,' said Barbara, remembering, and wishing that she did not, a far less discriminating and un-impassioned Marquês.

'No, he's always been the soul of chivalry. Rather too much so, to be honest,' said Pepita, once again relapsing into her old character. 'It made me nervous. But then, when he was talking about the wedding, he put his arms round me and we talked about how long we had known each other and how surprised some of our friends would be because we'd never been anything but friends ourselves, and he said they thought...' She stopped with another of her quick, calculating looks. 'It just seemed wrong, somehow,' she finished. 'We didn't belong together.' Her voice was suddenly absolutely sober, without affectation or any sort of calculation. 'We were friends, but we didn't belong together like that. Do you understand?'

Barbara felt as if she had received a second, crueller blow. She would have liked to deny knowledge of what Pepita was talking about. But she was not good at lying, and something in the Spanish girl's face told her she already knew the answer.

'Yes, I understand that,' she agreed reluctantly.

Pepita gave her a brilliant smile, as if she were relieved of a great burden.

'So you will help me? You will go to Ruy and explain? Take his ring back? Tell him that I made a mistake?'

Barbara's hazel eyes clouded with horror. 'I couldn't!'

But Pepita was positively blithe. 'Of course you can. It's the perfect answer. I knew that as soon as—er—I heard you were working in that agency.'

'No,' said Barbara with force, and plunged the coffee-cup down on to the small glass table with utterly uncharacteristic clumsiness.

Pepita did not believe her. For quite three minutes she prattled on about what a weight it was off her mind; where Barbara could find Ruy; how easy it would be to get in touch with him. Why, they could go and telephone now...

'No!' said Barbara again, with a note of desperation that even Pepita could not avoid hearing.

Pepita said blankly, 'What's the matter?'

Barbara looked round the crowded lounge. Nobody was looking at her, she found. That felt odd, because she felt as if she had been shouting, all her feelings exposed and raw. She would have given anything to be a hundred miles away. But this idea of Pepita's had to be dealt with.

She bit her lip. 'Look, Pepita, I haven't seen him for ages...'

'Ten years,' said Pepita, nodding.

'And when we parted, it wasn't very civilised.'

The Spanish girl stared at her. 'What do you mean...parted?' she echoed on a rising note. 'Are you saying that you and Ruy—you and Ruy—but you were a child...'

'I was eighteen,' Barbara said levelly.

Pepita dismissed this with a wave of a manicured hand. 'You were a child. We all knew it.' She paused, a look of real worry on her mobile face. 'Are you saying that when you ran away it was because of Ruy? I thought you'd had some sort of fight with that dreadful man your uncle picked up. It never occurred to me...'

Barbara realised with a sinking heart that she was going to have to tell Pepita everything. Briefly she closed her eyes. She had hoped that in time the

memory would fade, if she buried it in silence and
refused to think about it. Stupid, of course. One
did not forget a man like Ruy Nieves dos Santos;
or his contempt. She said in a low voice, 'Pepita,
if I tell you something, I want you to promise never
to speak of it.'

'I won't tell Ruy,' Pepita promised softly.

Barbara gave a choked laugh, so full of bitterness that her friend recoiled. 'That wasn't quite
what I meant. I don't want you to mention it to
me again, either. I—try to forget. And most of the
time I succeed.'

She moved her head in a gesture which was suddenly reminiscent of the much younger Barbara
Lamb. At eighteen she had had long hair, tumbling
to her waist, tied back with a scarf or an old bit of
ribbon. It was always gleaming with health and
fragrant with the shampoo she used, but its wildness
made her look slightly unkempt, like one of the
ragged ponies on which Pepita mounted her small
pupils. Now, just for a second, the uncertain,
shaggy teenager was visible in the poised woman
on the velvet sofa.

It was so long ago, and yet she had perfect recall:
of every time she had seen the Marquês Nieves dos
Santos, every chilling glance, every contemptuous
word, and then in the end the absolute devastation
of his final rejection. Yet there was more to the
story than that, and Barbara told it calmly, although
Pepita had to lean forward to catch the almost inaudible words, and once or twice she saw her flinch,
physically flinch, at some unspoken memory.

It had all begun with her uncle. 'Major' Harry Lamb—her father's brother—was a self-made man and a self-appointed soldier. The nearest Harry had come to the Army was stealing stores from lorries crossing Salisbury Plain, and a teenage niece had been an inconvenience to him. But after the deaths of his brother and his brother's wife Harry had saddled himself, as he put it, with fifteen-year-old Barbara and whisked her off to Europe, 'out of harm's way'. There they had kept on the move: the south of France, Spain, a time in Mexico, then back to Spain and eventually the Algarve.

Barbara squared her shoulders. 'Well, you remember the Algarve. I'd just had my eighteenth birthday when we arrived, and you and I met in our first week there.'

Pepita nodded.

'Harry had a number of jobs there. He cleaned pools. He served behind bars. He was caretaker of the villa where we met. And then he met Brian Gallaher.'

'I remember,' said Pepita, steel in her soft voice.

Brian Gallaher had been a property developer of sorts, and not a very scrupulous one. He had been trying to buy land cheap from the local people and then build villas to sell to foreigners for huge sums. Inevitably, Harry Lamb had become involved as a negotiator, and Brian Gallaher had come to stay.

Harry had by that time been deeply in debt to the brash businessman, but fortunately—for him—Gallaher had made no secret of his attraction to Harry's niece. So Harry and his current girlfriend had taken off for Spain, telling Barbara that

Gallaher was moving into the villa to protect her while they were away. It was for protection from Brian Gallaher that Barbara had fled to the *quinta* of the Marquês Nieves dos Santos.

'I ran,' she said without emotion. 'I simply fled from our terrace and down through the apricot trees and kept on running. Of course, the *quinta* was quite close. And I used to visit the Marquesa.'

'Ruy took you in?' said Pepita on a note of discovery. This was news to her.

'Eventually.' Barbara thought of telling her the events of that night and discarded the idea. 'Unfortunately, he thought I'd arranged for Gallaher to stay the night and simply got frightened when Gallaher got drunk. He—left me in no doubt what he thought of me.'

'No!' exclaimed Pepita in instinctive protest. 'Surely——'

Barbara lifted her shoulders. She was very pale, the fine bones of her face pronounced.

'It doesn't matter. He took me in, anyway. He wouldn't let them wake up the Marquesa, but he gave me a bed for the night. I—refused to go back to the villa and he—the Marquês—went to see Gallaher. He came back——' She clamped her mouth shut, remembering Ruy's clipped rage when he'd returned from that expedition, the twist of the marred mouth that had showed his contempt for her bewildered innocence. She had expected him to lose hold on his intimidating self-control and blast her with his anger, but he had simply bowed his handsome head in arctic courtesy and announced that he would be summoning her uncle back from his Spanish holiday at once. The next day, Harry had come.

Barbara said carefully, 'Harry—rather got the wrong idea. He accused him—the Marquês—of seducing me.' Even at the memory, her whole body jerked in shame. Ruy had looked at him incredulously, with such proud disdain that Barbara, who had secretly hero-worshipped his glittering green eyes and lithe figure, had found herself wanting to die.

'Harry was—a bit of an opportunist. He tried blackmail. He said that if he—the Marquês—paid him, he wouldn't tell. He'd even leave me there in the *quinta*. For him to do what he wanted with, I suppose.' Her voice was suddenly immensely weary. 'I've never seen anyone so angry.'

'Oh, God,' said Pepita, 'I had no idea.'

Barbara forced a smile. 'Well, no, I didn't tell you. I didn't tell anyone.'

'But Ruy wouldn't blame you. He couldn't!' Pepita sounded appalled. 'He knew perfectly well that you were still a child—— '

He hadn't kissed her that day as if she were a child, Barbara thought harshly, and saw with relief that Pepita was already so shocked that there would be no need to tell her the rest of it. There would be no need to relive that shattering scene with the Marquês Nieves dos Santos which had once seemed like the beginning of her life, and had turned out instead to be the bitterest of endings. As long as she lived, she would never forget the look of distaste on his face when his arms released her.

To cut the conversation short she said, 'He gave me money,' and found that the words hurt her throat.

'*Ruy* did? The dollars you had when you came to us?' Pepita stared at her. 'I always thought you'd got them from Gallaher.'

Barbara shook her head. 'No, they were my pay-off,' she said with bitter self-mockery. 'The Marquês paid me to go away. Now do you see why I can't go to him for you?'

It came as a slight shock, returning from the all too vivid past to the present: this over-civilised hotel, Pepita dressed like something out of one of the fashion magazines that Senhora Martinez used to study avidly, the bustle of people and the smell of coffee. And Pepita was unhappy.

She said, 'I've been very stupid. I should have realised . . .'

Barbara shook her head. 'About me and my little domestic tragedy? How could you?' Her mouth was wry. 'I tried hard enough to disguise it.'

Pepita said, 'When you came to the stables . . . you were running away from *Ruy*?'

'I was running away from everything,' said Barbara, recalling with a pang her distraught younger self.

'You didn't get in touch with your uncle? Make him explain to Ruy?' probed Pepita.

'What was there to explain? That he was ripping off Ruy's workers by buying their little plots of land for a tenth of their worth? And that, in the end, he had tried to cheat the Marquesa, too?' Barbara said in sudden bitterness.

Pepita looked shaken. 'Had he?'

'Apparently.' Barbara tried to sound indifferent. 'He—the Marquês—stopped him. Or so Harry told me.'

Pepita looked at her swiftly. 'You still see him?'

Barbara gave a short, unamused laugh. 'Oh yes, it's not easy to get rid of Harry. He sees me as his insurance policy. Every time he's short of money, he pops up. And, strictly speaking, I owe him. Apparently there was another crooked deal—a big one—which forced Harry out of England. It was my father's deal. So,' she shrugged, 'since my father's deal meant Harry had to lie low for a long time, I owe him the occasional handout. In fact,' she looked at her watch, 'I'd better be going back to work for just that reason. Harry cleaned me out again the last time he turned up, and I need this week's pay cheque. I don't want to give Trevor any excuse to fire me.'

Pepita frowned. 'I thought you were partners.'

'Trevor's the one with the capital,' said Barbara. 'So he signs the salary cheques.'

She got to her feet.

Pepita jumped up at once. 'Don't go. We have so much to talk about,' she said rapidly. 'You've changed. I didn't think . . .'

She had more social poise these days, Barbara noted remotely. Ten years ago she would have caught hold of Barbara's lapel and shaken her. For a moment the Spanish girl looked really panic-stricken.

It was a feeling with which Barbara could not help but sympathise, that fear of the Marquês. Had he not taught her to fear him herself?

Pepita said breathlessly, 'Please, Barbara, wait a minute—you don't understand.'

'Please——' said Barbara raggedly, and almost pushed her out of the way.

She knew that people looked at her as she hurried through the hotel lobby. She did not care. All that mattered was that she get away from the past, with its tentacles and its impossible demands.

CHAPTER TWO

IN THE OFFICE, Trevor was seething. Barbara barely noticed. He glared as she came in.

'That took long enough. I suppose you're working late tonight to make up the hours?' he said nastily.

'Yes,' she said, her voice absent.

It added fuel to his simmering sense of injury.

'Well, what sort of client is she? Did you get any contract offer?'

Barbara stared at him emptily.

'You're impossible!' exclaimed Trevor, bursting out of control. 'You think this office is just an extension of your home. You can have callers, telephone your decorator; I'm surprised you don't bring your knitting!'

'I don't knit,' said Barbara remotely. It was interesting; anger alarmed her, but in his anger Trevor was just ridiculous, whereas a few silent words, a still, carved face with that cruel scar branding it from cheekbone to lips, were terrifying in their anger even across the divide of ten years.

'We're running a business here, you know. We're professionals. We have to behave professionally, responsibly.'

Something snapped in Barbara's head. She put her briefcase down on the top of her desk very carefully.

'We do, indeed,' she said steadily. 'I'm glad you brought that up, Trevor. Dan and I have been worried about these new clients of yours that you're talking about. Are they shady?'

He was so utterly disconcerted, she could have laughed. His eyes narrowed to slits.

'Why do you say that?' he hedged.

Barbara sighed. 'Because I know you, Trevor. Who are they, and how big is your cut?'

Perhaps because he was thrown off balance, perhaps because he was secretly proud of himself, he told her. Barbara listened in mounting horror. It was not so different from one of Harry's schemes, sly and shabby. And, worst of all, the person from whom they were buying the land was an old lady, unworldly and trusting. Barbara remembered how Harry had gloated over his deal with the Marquesa before her grandson had stopped it. Disgust rose in her.

She said so, not mincing her words, and Trevor lost much of his bluster. He sat down truculently, but she could see that he was impressed. But he was not going to admit it.

'Fine words,' he said nastily, 'from someone who spent the whole morning having coffee with a schoolfriend.'

Barbara met his eyes steadily. In her mind's eye she could see Pepita's distraught face. She weighted it against Trevor's petulance and found where her priorities lay. Honesty and friendship, or a paltry career working for a man she neither liked nor trusted. She sighed. That fastidiousness of hers, as Harry often pointed out, would be her downfall.

This time it seemed as if it was going to ease her out of a salaried job.

She said coolly, 'Not only this morning. I'll be out this afternoon as well. She's asked me to do something, and I owe her. *I*,' just the faintest emphasis on the pronoun, but it made Trevor flush darkly, 'pay my debts.' She picked up her telephone. 'Rosemary, will you get me the Savoy, please? Miss Martinez' suite.'

The Nieves dos Santos house was in a pleasant crescent, behind a positive copse of trees and shrubs. As soon as she pushed open the ironwork gate, Barbara's smile disappeared and her heart contracted. The house looked friendly, a family house, for all its elegance. But Ruy Nieves dos Santos was not friendly. Elegant, yes; supremely elegant, with that spare, intelligent face and lithe body. Pleasant, too. He could certainly be pleasant if he chose, though his civility could bite, as she remembered all too well. But there was no friendship here for her and never would be, even if she had not been coming on this traitor's errand.

By the time her hesitant ring was answered, she was as taut as a bowstring. The complete indifference on the face of the woman who answered the door was something of an anticlimax.

She took Barbara's name without any emotion, and asked her to wait in the hall while she went to see whether the Marquês was at home. Shivering convulsively, Barbara sat on the very edge of a tapestry-covered chair, her fingers flexing over her shoulder-bag where the precious ring box was secreted. She felt slightly sick.

When the cool girl came back, she looked at Barbara with noticeably more interest. There was, however, no increase in her courtesy.

'You're to go in,' she said casually, and indicated the door at the end of the marble-tiled hallway.

Feeling as if she were going to her execution, Barbara went.

The room was a large one with a conservatory at one end, a curved Victorian structure with a conical roof that jutted out into the garden. Her first impression was that she had somehow walked right through the house and out into the woodland that surrounded it. Her second impression, a heart-stopping one, was that she had walked into a fairy story and found that the gentle Beast was quite as implacable as his reputation painted him, and any gentleness would be reserved for someone quite other than herself. In a gesture of which she was completely unaware, she clenched the hand on the strap of her shoulder-bag convulsively against her breast.

The silent, predatory man watching her from the sunlit conservatory noted the gesture, and his mouth tightened. It was an ugly movement, revealing in the brilliant sunshine that one side of his face was irreparably scarred with a line that swept savagely from the very edge of his eye to the corner of his mouth. It was a scar that made most people flinch the first time they saw it. Barbara did not flinch. But then Barbara, he reminded himself, had seen it many times and, once at least, closer than most people.

He came forward, lithe and silent. She was, he saw, shaking. She was very slender and very tense, the veins in her trembling hands clearly visible. He frowned quickly.

But all he said was, 'You wanted to see me?'

'Yes.' It was a thread of sound.

He waited, the strange, observant eyes watching her without blinking. She felt them on her like the presence of a flame before her, and her shaking increased. She cleared her throat, trying for a normal tone. 'Pepita asked me to come. Pepita Martinez.'

The Marquês inclined his head. His hair was still midnight-dark and glossy as an otter's fur, she thought. She recalled with a sudden wave of desolation what it had felt like to stroke that hair.

She said hurriedly, 'She wants you to know she's changed her mind.' It sounded awful put like that. Barbara tried again. 'I mean, she's thought about it and she's not certain. No, I don't mean that. She's certain that it wouldn't work. She's sorry,' she added conscientiously.

Her host did not speak. The unnerving eyes had never left her. She stirred, then she thrust a hand into her bag and drew out the jeweller's box.

The Marquês did not even look at it. He received it from her fingers, not taking his eyes from her face. The touch of their skin seemed not to affect him at all, thought it made Barbara jump as if she had been scalded.

He disengaged himself at once, casting the box away from him on to a side table as if it were a thing of no significance. Then he snapped his glance away. Barbara felt her knees sag as if she had been released from torture, and she hurriedly sat down before her knees gave out. The Marquês did not appear to notice that she had subsided on one of his beautiful Second Empire sofas. He was frowning, the thin brows drawn into a straight line, so that he looked both fierce and dangerous.

The prolonged silence was chilling. Barbara had to clench her hands hard in her lap to prevent herself fidgeting. She looked everywhere but at the cold, closed face. There was no sound but the heavy ticking of the carriage clock on the mantelpiece behind him. When at last he spoke, she almost jumped.

'Why you?' demanded the Marquês harshly.

He was not looking at her. He was staring ahead of him, through the luxuriant plants and glass walls of the conservatory, as if he could not see them. His profile was elegant, but the scar which marred the left side of his face pulled the beautiful mouth down into a perpetual sneer. Barbara repressed a shiver.

'Pepita felt that it would be easier if you did not meet at this juncture,' she said carefully.

The Marquês gave a bark of laughter. 'You mean she chickened out,' he said, the schoolboy slang failing to disguise the anger which licked through the words.

'I—er—I think she was afraid you might try to persuade her to marry you against her better judgement,' she murmured, remembering the Spanish girl's shaking figure and white face when

she had handed over the ring. It had surprised her—
and convinced her that her quixotic decision was
right, after all.

The Marquês whipped round to face her, his
expression mocking.

'Persuade her?' he mimicked savagely. 'Seduce
her? Bully her? Beat her up? You don't have to
pretty it up for me, Barbara Lamb. I know exactly
what people say about me. But I thought Pepita
knew better.'

With his back to her he said, almost under his
breath, 'And why in God's name did she have to
make you her messenger?'

She said bitterly, 'I've been wondering that
myself.'

The Marquês said abruptly. 'Where is she?'

Barbara was alarmed. 'You're not going to try
to see her? I promised...'

He gave her a wolfish smile. 'Did you promise
to keep me away from her?'

She could not meet the glittering eyes. She looked
away.

'Ah, you did. How rash!'

Barbara swallowed. 'I said I would *ask* you...
Pepita is very unhappy.'

'Are you appealing to my chivalry?' He sounded
incredulous, even amused.

She said waspishly, because she was frightened,
'I know they say it's a lost cause, but you must
have *some* feeling for Pepita. You were going to
marry her. Surely you don't want her to be
unhappy?'

He was watching her. Eventually he shrugged.

'Pepita doesn't seem too concerned about *my* happiness. Why should I be any different?' he said coolly.

Because Ruy was not pale and shaking and on the edge of hysteria. Because, though he was annoyed, Ruy did not look as if he was facing the end of the world. Because Ruy was in every sense stronger and more self-reliant than Pepita Martinez.

Barbara said steadily, 'You could afford to be generous.'

The eyes, the strange greenish eyes that she had never forgotten, slashed over her. She stepped back as if he had flourished a sword blade, then found he was laughing.

'Generous? I?' he mocked.

'You could,' she insisted. 'Pepita is convinced that you would—er—make each other unhappy. That you're not right for each other. But her mother won't listen. You're the only hope of help she has. She feels...'

'She feels ashamed,' he interjected swiftly.

Barbara stared at him, and his mouth twisted.

'Don't look at me like that. Do you think I don't know Pepita very well? And yet, as you say, I was going to marry her. No, you don't have to explain the girl to me. I know exactly what she's feeling now.' Although his voice was light, almost bored, Barbara heard the anger.

She bit her lip, but said softly, 'Then show some pity.'

He flinched; she saw it with interest and almost disbelief.

'She was very clever to send you.'

Barbara was silent. His smile became more twisted, but he did not expand on his ironic murmur. At last he gave a quick shrug and came with his characteristic quick, light step to the table where she was standing.

'What do you want me to do?' He sounded resigned.

'Cancel the wedding. Talk to her mother. Forgive her.'

He put a hand over his scarred eye. 'Very well.' He seemed tired, almost indifferent.

Barbara stared. After his anger, she had expected fury, reproaches, threats. This quiet acquiescence unnerved her. She looked at him narrowly. His face was drawn, but quite expressionless. He looked down at the square velvet ring box for a long moment, not touching it.

Then, unexpectedly, he said, 'I suppose it was never going to work.'

To her astonishment, Barbara felt tears well behind her eyes. She shook her head a little. Ruy Nieves dos Santos did not need her sympathy or anyone else's. He strode through the world doing exactly what he wanted, no matter whom he hurt in the process, and he deserved everything he got.

She said more baldly than she intended, 'Then why did you try to make her?'

For a moment he looked astonished. Then his face closed again, and he was laughing, spreading his hands in an exaggerated gesture of helplessness.

'It was fate.'

She glared at him. It was easier than feeling the sympathy he did not merit and certainly did not want. 'Don't be ridiculous!'

'But it is true. I—needed a wife. And Pepita— or so she assured me—wanted to marry. She knew my family, my circumstances. It seemed the perfect solution.'

He could not have sounded more uncaring if he were talking about a pound of fish, Barbara thought with dislike. She wondered why, after all these years, he needed a wife, and supposed, cynically, that he had found he had dynastic urges after all, in spite of his very public preference for bachelorhood. Pepita, she thought, was well out of it. It was very clear that he had never intended to change his way of life. Pepita had been, as he said, a solution, a convenience. And if he were in love with her—as for a moment Barbara had been wholly and compassionately sure he was—it would be beneath his dignity ever to admit it.

She averted her eyes, horrified at the trend of her thoughts. It seemed an intrusion to know so much about his private life that he did not know she knew.

She said stiffly, 'I've done my errand. I must go.'

'And wash your hands of the whole distasteful matter?' he queried mockingly.

Her colour deepened. 'It's none of my business...'

His eyes had narrowed, she saw from beneath her lashes. She could not look him in the face.

'Don't you think you've made it your business, coming here like this?'

Oh God, so he was angry. He saw her message-carrying as interference. That apparent indifference was just his old, well-bred social mask. Barbara quailed.

'Pepita asked me...'

'And of course you couldn't turn her down.' How could a voice that was so smooth sound so savage?

Forgetting her embarrassment, she looked at his face. He sounded furious and also oddly satisfied, as if he had been given proof of a crime whose solution he had long suspected. Meeting the cool green eyes, Barbara winced.

He saw it, and the beautiful, sensual mouth twisted suddenly.

'You can't bear to look at me, can you?' he said.

Barbara swallowed. There was not much point in denying it when she knew that her face gave her away. Absently he touched his scar. It was a familiar gesture. Ten years ago he had had the habit of running one finger along its length while he contemplated an opponent. She had only been an opponent once, but she remembered seeing him doing it while he talked to others; and of course she could never forget that incident herself.

The Marquês said impatiently, 'Don't look so startled. You're not the only one who doesn't like this face of mine.' He paused and then said mockingly, 'I'm not wild about it myself. But—unlike you—I have to live with it.'

For some reason—no reason she could identify—Barbara felt her heart lurch. It was if they were on a raft which had been hit by unexpected surging waves. She looked even more startled. Their eyes locked, hers wide and faintly alarmed, his mocking.

She pulled herself together.

'I'm sorry if you feel I've—intruded,' she said quietly. 'I—didn't think. I thought I was helping.' Her smile was crooked. 'I'll go now.'

'No!' It came at her like a shot, like a blow.

Swiftly he moved across the room, almost as if he would bar her way. Barbara was bewildered. She turned, following him, wanting now only to get away out of his disturbing presence and the memories that his every gesture unleashed.

He was standing in full sunlight, his eyes fixed on her. The scar was cruelly illuminated, giving him a sinister, vengeful appearance.

She set her teeth. It was silly to think like that. What did he have to revenge? If anyone had a score to settle, it was herself, and she did not want to. She did not want to bring up anything of the past. All she wanted was to escape with as little damage as possible.

In the bright sunlight the Marquês' eyes were naked, ablaze with some emotion she could not guess at, did not want to guess at.

'At least let me give you whatever it is you take at this time of day,' he said rapidly, his eyes not leaving her. He pressed a bell in the wall beside him. 'Tea, I suppose? Or something stronger?'

She had no time to reply before the door opened and he was throwing a casual order at the girl who appeared. She had gone before Barbara had time to protest.

He gestured to the sofa behind her.

'Really, I'd better be going,' she said, standing her ground. 'I've got to get back to work.'

He came over to her. Barbara backed, finding herself sitting down without ever intending to do so. She had forgotten how tall Ruy was, she thought confusedly; how intimidating in his height. That was what it was that made her heart race like this, the simple instinct of one animal retreating from another that was bigger and more powerful.

His eyes narrowed at that reflex retreat of hers, but he said nothing. Instead he flung himself into a gold brocade armchair, watching her. 'It's been a long time,' he said abruptly.

Though it cost her to do so, Barbara met his eyes candidly. 'Ten years.'

'A little over,' he corrected.

'Y-yes, I suppose so.'

'You haven't changed much.'

She was amazed. She had changed beyond all recognition. Her mirror told her so, her Uncle Harry told her so; even Pepita had dimly perceived that she was not the shivering adolescent she had been.

Wryly, Ruy smiled. 'You've cut your hair, and got into clothes that fit you. The essentials haven't changed.'

Barbara's constraint evaporated in sheer surprise. 'Of course I've changed. I was like a shaggy pony. You used to hate it.'

He raised his brows. 'I did?'

She glared at him in ancient resentment. 'You told the Marquesa I wasn't to wear shorts in the *quinta*.'

For a moment he was blank, then unforgivably amused. His eyes swept over her, laughing. 'I remember. But I don't remember saying I hated it.'

She hunched a shoulder. 'You weren't very kind.'

He surveyed her, his eyes unreadable again. At last he said slowly, as if he was making a discovery, 'I don't suppose I was.'

'*And* you were rude about my hair,' pursued Barbara rancorously.

'I?' He was laughing again. 'What did I say?'

But she had remembered with disastrous clarity not only the insult, but the circumstances in which it had been delivered. Her hands clenched on the seat of the sofa. She was almost certain, from his soft laugh, that he too remembered the detail.

'You shouldn't let that mop fly free,' he taunted her softly. They had been in his car, that dashing vehicle that proclaimed his status as the rich playboy; it was open-topped and as it had swung round a corner the veering air currents had whipped it across his face. He had, much against his will, been driving her back from a visit to his grandmother. 'Why don't you put it in plaits like the child you are?'

She flinched from that too precise, too vivid memory.

'But I didn't,' he reminded her, 'say I didn't like it. Just that it was a danger to my driving.' He paused. 'Why did you cut it?'

Barbara shrugged again. 'I had to grow up some time.'

Instantly his face was taut. 'By God, you did!'

The door opened and a tubby man with a friendly face appeared, bearing a tray. For a moment Barbara did not recognise him. Then, in disbelief, she said, 'Pedro?'

He smiled at her. '*Senhorinha.*'

But he was not as uncomplicatedly glad to see her as he had been in the old days. He poured tea and handed it to her. It was pale gold with a smoky perfume, served in exquisite porcelain. The subtlety of the brew and the delicacy of the china reminded her of how clumsy she had always felt in the Marquesa's perfect house; clumsy and out of place. The feeling returned now.

The Marquês appeared not to notice. He drank his own tea as if it were water, throwing it down his throat with a sort of leashed impatience that embarrassed Barbara. If he had another appointment that he was so anxious to go to, why on earth had he insisted on this ridiculous ceremony of refreshment?

As Pedro closed the door softly behind him, she said once more, 'I really must go soon. My job...'

'This estate agency?'

She was surprised. But then she realised that Pepita must have told him where she worked. She nodded.

'You have been there long?'

'Some time,' she said coolly, not liking his tone.

'You have known him long, this employer?'

'I worked with him before we set up the agency,' she told him, putting down her cup. She gathered her bag into her hands. 'Thank you for the tea. 'I must...'

'So he's not an old *personal* friend?' The Marquês persisted.

'Personal?'

'A friend of the family. Of your uncle's, for example?'

'They've never met,' she snapped.

'No? You haven't introduced them? He is not, then, your lover?'

'My...' For a moment Barbara was speechless.

'You are a director of his business,' the Marquês pointed out.

She glared at him. 'Why the cross-examination? Yes, I'm a director. I helped to form the agency. I'm one of the management team. That doesn't mean that we're...that Trevor...'

'Has made you his mistress,' the Marquês supplied in a drawl.

She said coldly, 'That's a very old-fashioned phrase.' She wondered whether he was punishing her, taking a subtle revenge from her own unwilling invasion of his private life. 'And it's none of your business, any more than your affairs are mine. I've already apologised for that. What more can I do?' She lifted her eyes, her expression between indignation and pleading.

He scanned her expression, then he gave a soft laugh.

'Reparation?' he said thoughtfully. 'Well, why not? Let's have a forfeit.'

Barbara felt a twinge of her earlier alarm. 'I didn't mean...'

'Have dinner with me tonight,' he said, ignoring her protest. 'We have a lot to catch up on,' he reminded her.

She gave a little shiver, but she said stoutly, 'Oh no, we don't.'

'And you haven't finished explaining to me why Pepita sent you to conduct this delicate negotiation. Nor,' he finished softly, 'have I given you my answer to take her.'

Barbara stared at him, then she looked pointedly at the glittering box on the table beyond them. 'I don't see what answer is necessary.'

'Don't you?' His smile was devilish. 'But I'm sure Pepita is very anxious that I should not make a scandal.' His smile grew as he saw Barbara's face. 'For myself, I don't care. There have been so many scandals in my life.' He was running his thumb along the scar, as if he were feeling the cutting edge of a dagger. Once again Barbara had a vivid picture of him ten years ago. It was dizzying in its intensity. He was looking at her calmly, measuringly, as if she were his opponent this time.

'But I might be prepared to do the chivalrous thing. Especially if,' he explained as she still did not respond, 'I am persuaded.' His eyes held hers compellingly. It had the inevitability of a dream—or, thought Barbara, surrendering to the implacability she saw in his face, a nightmare. It hardly surprised her. He gave her a sudden charming smile. 'So have dinner with me tonight and persuade me,' he said.

CHAPTER THREE

NOTWITHSTANDING her sense of fatalism, Barbara dressed for dinner with the Marquês with the utmost care. By the time she had finished, her bed was littered with discarded garments and her hair had been rearranged ten times or more.

She had not the remotest guess where he would take her to dine. In the Algarve he had never taken her out. Nor, as far as she could remember the gossip, had he ever been seen dining with anyone else in one of the many restaurants in the area. He had eaten at the *quinta*, shunning the public haunts, even the most exclusive.

Wherever he took her, she did not want to be conspicuous. So she emptied her wardrobe in search of inconspicuous good taste, and ended with a result that did not begin to satisfy her.

She teamed a pale linen suit with her one good blouse, heavy figured satin, the colour of ripe conkers. It mirrored her shining hair, all the copper lights in it brought out by the gorgeous colour. She shook her head at herself in the looking-glass. Inconspicuous? She glowed like an autumn fire. And it was not just the colours: her whole face had come alive.

She tried to subdue it with more make-up than she normally used. It was hopeless.

In the mirror her image looked back at her, large-eyed and glimmering with excitement. The smooth hair had been combed and swirled into a sophisticated upswept style, which left her ears and throat vulnerably exposed. She clipped on topaz drop earrings, hoping they would make her look more sophisticated. But she could do nothing about the delicate colour in her cheeks or the brightness of her eyes. Nor could she subdue the faint, revealing tremulousness of her mouth.

She leaned closer to the glass. In fact, that mouth gave her away completely. She scrubbed at the gloss she had applied, but it had no effect other than to leave her lips rosier than before.

'Damn,' said Barbara with dislike to the too youthful, too vulnerable girl in the mirror.

She set off, thoroughly ruffled.

She had refused to allow the Marquês to collect her. She felt she needed to keep her address, her home, private from him. She had expected a fight, but he had acquiesced almost absently. And now she was making her own way to his house.

She was a little late, but she still dawdled, aware that she did not want to reach her destination. That was unusual for her. Normally she made almost a fetish of promptness. It would not worry the Marquês, she knew. Awareness of time was not a strong Portuguese trait, in her experience, and had been less developed in the Marquesa than in most.

She was surprised, therefore, when the Marquês himself opened the door to her, before she had even raised her hand to ring the bell, and almost pounced on her.

'Where have you been? Have you had an accident? Missed your way?'

'I—miscalculated the time,' she said lamely with a surreptitious look at her watch.

He seemed to take hold of himself.

'We'll be a little late, but I don't suppose it matters. But come along now.'

And, without letting her set foot over the threshold, he urged her back down the path to where a large limousine was parked. Barbara took it in with mixed feelings. It was evident that, wherever they were going, the Marquês did not intend to drive himself. So private conversation in the car was out of the question.

Pedro smiled at her over his shoulder as the Marquês himself helped her into the car and then swept round for low-voiced instructions to his chauffeur. Barbara saw Pedro nod, then get into the car as the Marquês swung his long legs in beside her. And then they were purring silently through the London traffic and out, into the sunset, on the motorway.

Barbara looked at the man beside her under her lashes. He seemed perfectly relaxed, but something—she did not know what—told her that he was on edge, tense and braced as if for an ordeal. For a moment she had a horrid suspicion that he was going to ask her to beg Pepita to change her mind. Then one glance at that stern profile made her revise the thought. He was not a man who begged, even when his whole happiness was at stake.

She swallowed and said the first thing that came into her head.

'Where are we going?'

He glanced down at her. 'I wondered when you'd ask that. I could, of course, be kidnapping you. Whisking you off to Portugal with me.'

Barbara laughed, partly in relief. This was the sort of banter she could cope with. 'Not unless we're going by way of Bristol and points west,' she said.

'Ah, a good sense of direction—rare in women.'

'I can read the signposts,' she pointed out tartly.

He laughed. 'So I haven't found the first female map-reader in history!'

She sniffed. 'That's sexist. Women are as good at reading maps as men. I doubt,' she added darkly, 'that anyone of either sex is very good at it if they're having questions barked at them by someone drumming his fingers on the steering wheel.'

He turned his head, stretching his legs out before him, and regarded her lazily.

'You think you know me very well, don't you, little Barbara?'

He had not called her 'little Barbara' in that tone of voice before, not even ten years ago. She sat up very straight.

'I don't know you at all,' she said. 'And I don't want to. Where are we going?'

He gave a soft laugh but answered obediently. 'You remember Dick and Alanna?'

She winced. They were a young couple who had run the inn on the Bandeirante development. Dick had employed her to serve behind the bar sometimes. It was he who, furious with embarrassment, had first warned her about the trouble that Harry would get himself into if he took on the Marquês Nieves dos Santos. In those days she had not understood what he was talking about.

'I see you do.'

She squared her shoulders against the unaccustomed luxury of leather upholstery. 'Of course.'

'Well, they returned to England a couple of years ago. They run a country house hotel by the river.'

'Is it doing well?' she asked politely.

His lips quirked. 'Very,' he said with equal politeness. 'They're booked every night, they tell me. The restaurant is already quite famous.'

'So how did you get a reservation at such short notice?' she asked drily. 'Your famous money and influence again?'

He shook his dark head, laughing, refusing to take offence at her waspishness.

'Shareholder's perks. I put some money into it. They always—er—accommodate me.'

'So what else is new?' muttered Barbara.

He swung round, sliding one arm along the back of the seat behind her.

'You always objected to people giving me service. Even then.' He did not sound angry, he sounded curious. 'Why?'

Barbara met his eyes straight on. She could not think of denying it. It was true. He had a right to an answer, if she knew it.

She said slowly, 'I suppose because you *expected* it somehow. You never had to *try*...'

His strange eyes glinted, green and yellow like a cat's in firelight. He shook his head. 'You're right, you don't know me. I never *tried* as you put it, so hard in my whole life as I did that damnable summer...'

He stopped and turned his face away from her. She could feel the tension in him like a third presence in the back of the car with them. At last he gave a small laugh and shrugged.

'Well, it's a long time ago now. Tell me what you've been doing in the meantime.'

Barbara gave him a brief sketch of her life: the struggle for qualifications, a decent job, the late-night study and the constant battle against poverty. And now the heights she had gained of her own small flat without flatmates who took all the hot water or returned noisily at three in the morning. Ruy laughed at her reminiscences and was thoughtful when she described her efforts to remedy the years of neglected education.

'You obviously have a very strong will,' he commented.

Barbara laughed. 'I don't like being beaten,' she agreed.

He narrowed his eyes at her. 'No, I can see that. Does that mean you are ambitious? Professionally ambitious?'

'I want a good job,' Barbara said after a moment's thought. 'I don't care whether I end up with my photograph in the gazette and my name on the notepaper.'

The Marquês nodded quickly. 'I understand completely. We are alike in that. We like to finish what we have started.'

Barbara looked at him quickly, but he was staring into the middle distance, his mouth oddly rigid. There did not seem to be any unpalatable hidden meaning to his words.

'So you're happy where you are? Not after a bigger and better agency?' And, as Barbara hesitated, he said sharply, 'Well?'

She bit her lip. 'Not a bigger one. Better, maybe.'

The slim brows flew up.

'I'm not sure I like some of the business Trevor is doing,' Barbara said, half to herself. 'And still less the way he's doing it.'

Ruy looked at her sharply, but all he said was, 'Difficult.'

Barbara turned to him. 'And you, *senhor*? What have you been doing since we last met?'

'*Senhor*?' he murmured, the mocking note back in his voice. But he allowed himself to be deflected easily enough into social anecdote.

He grew more serious when he mentioned his brother, however. 'The crash was a great shock to all of us. Lauren's parents have never really recovered. I took the boy, of course, but...'

'But...?' asked Barbara.

They were speeding along between rolling fields, which glimmered in the evening light like a patchwork in an infinity of greens. It was beautiful. Barbara felt that the serenity was almost unearthly, as if they were travelling through time as well as space, and were suspended somewhere unreal where they could meet as equals without the shadow of past or future to distort their confidences.

He gave an expressive shrug. 'It doesn't really answer. For one thing, Luis can't bear my face either.'

'*What?*' She was honestly shocked.

His laugh was harsh. 'It is not so surprising. He's very young, only just into his teens. He hasn't learned to disguise his feelings yet.'

'Could you be mistaken?' Barbara ventured, unbearably touched.

Ruy looked out at the perfect landscape.

'No,' he said bleakly.

'But surely, if he's young he'll get used ...'

'Barbara, he can't bear to look at me,' the Marquês said quietly. 'He looks anywhere else: the ceiling, the window, the plate in front of him. When I come into a room, he leaves as soon as he can. If I send for him, when he comes into the study, he looks sick.'

She put out a hand in pure instinct and touched the rigid fingers on his knee. He flinched, and she drew her hand away at once.

'I try to avoid him, of course,' the Marquês said heavily. 'There's no point in torturing the poor child. But I have to go to the *quinta* sometimes. And it's not always possible to arrange for him to visit somewhere else when I do.'

Barbara looked at the hawklike profile. 'I'm sorry,' she said helplessly.

He shrugged. For a moment his face was inscrutable. The scar was turned away from her, and she realised with a little start that before his injury he must have been startlingly handsome. It had never occurred to her before. Arrested, she looked at him as if for the first time, discovering the classical balance of cheekbone and eye-socket, the almost too perfect mouth. It was a face out of the sixteenth century—one of the ascetic navigator princes; scholar and courtier; scientist and poet. And lover?

Barbara swallowed, glad that the Marquês was not looking at her. A shiver of heat ran under her skin and she shifted uncomfortably as the car turned off the wide road.

They rode in silence after that until they reached their destination. When they turned into the driveway, Barbara caught her breath in undisguised delight.

'It was an Edwardian villa,' the Marquês told her. 'A ruin when Dick found it, though fortunately the glass was all intact. I think you'll like the restorations. And the view is splendid.'

There were one or two cars already there—long, low expensive things that looked as if there were chauffeurs to go with them somewhere about the place. The front door stood open from the well-lit porch, but the Marquês ignored it. Instead he guided her along a jasmine-arched path beside the house to the lawns behind.

Stopping, Barbara caught her breath.

'Yes,' he said with quiet satisfaction.

It was a perfect evening, that soft grey hour between sunset and nightfall when the air is full of the scents of blossom and fireflies appear. There were three lawns, each lower and longer than the last, which stretched down to the riverbank. On the lowest there were ironwork tables. It was clearly the focus of the cocktail hour. A pleasant hum floated up to them.

Ruy touched her elbow, indicating the mossy path which led away from the house. As in a dream, Barbara gave a little sigh and surrendered to the magic of it. A discreet waiter seated them on a rustic seat under a willow and brought drinks and cordon bleu canapés, while they studied menus the size of a medieval charter.

When they had chosen, and the bowing waiter had retreated, the Marquês lit one of his thin cigars, ignoring the food, though Barbara nibbled a tiny triangle of cheese puff pastry. Ruy inhaled and then blew a stream of smoke straight up into the air above his head. In the clear air it hovered above them. The sharp smell reminded Barbara of the *quinta* and the alien scents of his study: leather, woodsmoke and the pungent shadow of his cheroots. In spite of herself, in spite of the idyllic scene, she tensed.

He looked at her swiftly.

'Cold?'

She shook her head.

'We could go in,' he persisted.

'No.'

Deliberately she put the ten-year shadow away from her. She gave him a wry smile and he raised his brows.

'It's too beautiful to go in before we have to,' she said. 'Even worth getting cold.'

He followed her gesture at the magical garden, the little stream. His eyes were grave in the dusk. Barbara tilted her head back to look at the sky. It was very distant, studied with a thousand diamond chips that blurred as she stared at them. She felt light-headed and unlike herself.

'You know,' she said slowly, 'I feel as if this is— out of time. Do you understand that?'

He drew on his cigar. 'I'm not sure,' he drawled at last. 'Explain.'

'As if I've been given a chance to go through the looking-glass,' she said, musing. 'A sort of dispensation, if you like. I don't have to be sensible, not here and now. As if I've been let out of prison and—oh, licensed to do spontaneously whatever takes my fancy.'

There was a long silence. The shadows closed in. Behind them the voices of the other people on the terrace sank to murmurs.

At last Ruy said, 'Prison?' in an odd voice.

Barbara said, 'Only as a figure of speech.'

He smiled. 'Yes, I understand that. But——' he hesitated '—you do not normally allow yourself to be spontaneous?'

She shook her head vigorously, the silky hair stirring against her cheek with the movement. 'It's too much of a luxury.'

There was a sharp silence, as if he were turning her words over and over in his mind. Then he said, 'I think perhaps you have changed more than I thought.'

She moved uneasily, wanting to challenge the statement, wanting equally hard to stop him, but both conflicting wishes were thwarted by the return of the waiter. Their table was ready. Whenever they would like to eat . . .

The Marquês ground out his cigar and gave her his hand in a courteous, meaningless gesture. Reluctantly Barbara accepted it. They went up the darkening path hand in hand, like lovers.

The restaurant was in what must have been the Edwardian family's drawing-room and conservatory. There were more people here and the noise was louder. Barbara looked round, realising with a faint sense of unreality that she had never been to such a place before. At one end of the room there was a large party, the men in dinner-jackets, the women bright with satin and jewels. In a discreetly shaded corner she saw a famous face she knew from her television screen. And everywhere there was that air of careless elegance that does not count the cost. She felt the smile tilt her lips as she followed the waiter to their table.

'You are laughing,' the Marquês said softly.

She shook her head again. He watched her as if fascinated. Although she was plainly dressed, her hair shone as brilliantly as any of the diamonds in the room. The candles on the snowy cloth were reflected in her hazel eyes. She looked wondering and faintly mischievous. 'Only at myself.'

'Why?'

Her smile grew. 'You *shall* go to the ball, Cinderella.'

The thin brows snapped together. 'You're no Cinderella. Don't put yourself down.'

Barbara laughed again, happily. 'Cinderella,' she said firmly. 'On a trip to the moon and loving every minute of it. Don't spoil the illusion.'

Ruy relaxed. He made her a mocking little bow. 'Very well, we will both inhabit a fairy-tale—for tonight.'

And after that he set out to charm her. The charm was almost palpable, subtle and elegant, binding her in a web of warmth and wine and shared laughter.

They had a discreet corner table beside glass doors that opened on to the terrace and the scented night. The heady perfume of jasmine and old roses wafted round them. Behind them, the voices of their fellow diners rose and fell, unheeded. Across the tremulous candle flame, the cool green eyes held hers.

Barbara felt as if she were being lured out to sea, urged by a stronger, more confident mariner than herself. Half alarmed at her own daring, half entranced, she felt herself following Ruy into the depths. The restaurant conversation receded. There was no one else in the whole cool and infinitely exciting universe but the two of them. She shivered, not with cold.

The waiter came, served coffee and brandy with murmurous discretion, and evaporated from the real world. Neither of them had even noticed him. Barbara found she was staring into Ruy's eyes as if he were hypnotising her.

He said her name under his breath.

A little shudder of pure desire rippled up her spine and she sat straighter. What was that? Desire? *Desire*? For *this* man? It couldn't be real. It was all part of the illusion in which she was floating.

But there was a blaze in the green eyes, no longer cool, that was no illusion. Not quite believing it, she watched him put out a hand across the table to her. It was a demand. In a dream she put her own into it, feeling the long fingers close hard round it. The slender fingers flinched, as if he would crack the bones with the force of his possession. Barbara's mouth was dry. He leaned forward.

'Stay with me,' he said urgently. 'Here. Tonight.'

CHAPTER FOUR

THE OFFICE was airless. At eight in the morning it was also deserted, for which Barbara was grateful. She had not slept after her return to London last night, and in desperation had given up and walked through the diamond-bright streets in the early morning. If she could not sleep, at least she could work; maybe it would stop her remembering.

She ploughed her way doggedly through the pile of work that Trevor had left her. There was more of it than he had any right to expect her to do. But she did it, anyway. It had its uses. And all too soon it was finished.

She got up and went over to the coffee machine, catching sight of her own image in the glass above it. She did not look like herself. Her face had sharpened, somehow, so that she looked nervy and pinched, her mouth too tense and her eyes too big. She pressed the back of her fist against her mouth until it hurt. That was how she had looked last night: shocked and blank, as if she had been wrought to fever pitch, and then exploded.

She poured coffee, noting absently that there was still a tremor in her hands. She tried to tell herself it was the result of unaccustomed alcohol, but she did not believe it. Whatever she had done, whatever she had felt last night, she could not blame it on the wine. She had been intoxicated, all right, she

thought grimly, but not with the rare vintages that
the Marquês had commanded.

She looked at her pallor with dislike and sat
down. Well, it was over. *Please* let it be over. He
would not seek her out again. Not after...

And anyway, he did not know where she lived.
She had been reminding herself of that ever since
she had closed the door behind her last night. Ruy
had sent her home in his limousine, presumably re-
maining himself in the room that the obliging management had conjured for them at his softly voiced
request. Shame lashed her at the memory. She put
her coffee down and dropped her head in her hands.
She did not think she would ever forget it: not a
syllable, not a tense, flickering second.

He had accomplished it all so easily. In retrospect it was almost unbelievable how readily the
room had been made available, the key produced,
though at the time it had had a dreamlike inevitability Barbara had not even questioned.

They had gone up the shallow, blue-carpeted
staircase under the incurious gaze of the hotel re-
ceptionist. If she had thought about it, she would
have realised it was not the first time the Marquês
had stayed there; probably not the first time he had
persuaded a lady to stay with him in exactly the
same circumstances. But, with her fingers gripped
by his, Barbara had not been thinking. She had
gone with him blindly.

The room, as she saw it briefly, did not look like
a hotel suite. It was furnished in Edwardian style,
with light oak cupboards and chintz hangings in
tones of moonlit woods. The elaborate glass lamp

on the bedside table cast the only muted light in the room, before Ruy took her into his arms and she saw nothing behind her closed lids but the leaping flames of her own blood.

She had known how it would be, of course. After ten years her flesh had not forgotten the impression of his. She fitted into his arms as if she had never been out of them.

Ruy's mouth was harsh on hers. She remembered that, too. He was muttering, half sentences in his own language which she did not follow. Once, holding her face between his hands and looking deeply into her dazed eyes, he said her name.

Had she said anything? She must have done, surely. She could not just have clung to him, limp and acquiescent with delight. Because it had been a delight to feel his mouth on her brow, her quivering eyelids, her exposed throat; delight to give herself into those firm hands; delight to touch skin against skin.

In her office, Barbara clenched her fingers into her hair until she was dragging mercilessly at the scalp. No, in all that whirling pleasure she could not remember saying a thing. Certainly she had not protested.

So she could not really blame him. She had not said no, not in words, certainly not with her eager body, curving pliantly to his.

She shut her eyes tight as the unwelcome pictures flashed before her, undeniable and horribly vivid. She had never seen his dark hair disarranged before, but it had fallen turbulently across his brow: he'd shaken it impatiently out of his eyes as he bent to her. Her hands had been pale against the even tan of his chest. He had looked younger, eager—the beautiful mouth for once unguarded. She had been his, utterly his, and he had known it. The exultant green eyes had told her so.

Yet it had been he, in the end, who had hesitated. With Barbara abandoned in his arms, clinging to him, drawing his mouth to her own, he had paused.

'Barbara—little one—are you sure?' The slurred uneven voice was hardly his.

She stared, still locked in the fairy story, not understanding.

Ruy began to spread her gleaming hair carefully across one pillow, stroking it away from her face with gentle movements that were not quite steady. He avoided her eyes. He was leaning on one elbow, looking down at her.

'Is this really what you want? I—have to be sure.'

The scar was very evident. A tiny pulse at the corner of his eye throbbed, throwing the disfigurement into cruel relief. Barbara looked at it, her eyes filling with instinctive tears. His shoulders seemed to stiffen.

'Why?' she said softly, bewildered.

He misunderstood her. 'Because I'm not going to seduce you,' he told her. 'You do what you want to do. But you do it of your own free will.'

She stared at him, her skin slowly chilling. He seemed not to notice.

'You were talking about illusions earlier. About behaving spontaneously.' He drew a long breath. 'You said it was a luxury, and I agree with you.

But luxuries have their price. I just want to be sure you realise that.'

Barbara's arms fell away from him. Her lips felt icy.

'What are you saying?' she managed at last.

'Just that it's *your* decision. It's a price I can afford for myself, but not for anybody else. Do you understand me, Barbara? I'm not taking your decisions for you.'

He was saying that this was a casual attraction. He did not really want her except as a substitute for Pepita. Now it was she who could not meet his eyes, though he looked at her searchingly. She pushed him away, groping for her discarded clothes. It was an additional humiliation somehow that they had been scattered across the floor. She hunched over them as she pulled them on, her back to him. Ruy did not try to stop her.

The suite had a small bathroom, and she retreated into it. Her cheeks looked ashen in the thin light above the shaving mirror. She splashed cold water on to them and on to her wrists, but it did not seem to make any difference. She still looked as if she had been beaten.

When she went back he was dressed, though his shirt was unbuttoned and he had no tie. His jacket lay where they—no, where she—had thrown it, on a heavily cushioned armchair.

He looked at her gravely. Barbara fixed her eyes on a point just above his right ear and said clearly, 'I would like to go home, please.'

'You change your mind very quickly.'

'I doubt,' she said with precision and a bitterness that he could not mistake, 'that the mind has much to do with it.'

'Perhaps not. But couldn't you explain?' His tone was wry. Was he mocking her?

She flashed him a look verging on hatred.

'I would have thought it was obvious. You reminded me of the cost.'

The ascetic face closed. 'Too dangerous for you?'

Barbara shook her head vigorously. 'No. Just—not worth it.'

She thought he winced, but she could not be sure. He sat down very deliberately in the chintz chair and crossed one leg over the other. His whole pose was a mocking challenge.

'So you retreat back to that prison of yours? Freedom too frightening?' he jeered softly.

Barbara looked round the beautiful room with a shudder.

'This isn't freedom,' she said with conviction. 'This is pure fantasy. And I don't want any more of it. I don't know why you started it, Ruy, but I want it finished and done with. Now.'

'Why *I* started it?' he mused. 'I'm not sure that I did. Or not quite like that. It just—took hold.'

Barbara stared at him. His mouth twisted in that predator's grimace that his scar imposed.

'There was a lady,' he said almost to himself. 'And for a moment it seemed as if I wasn't alone any more. And then she panicked...'

He is talking about Pepita, Barbara thought, amazed at the pain. He stood up, came towards her. In unmistakable revulsion she stepped away, beating his reaching hands away. He said her name softly under his breath, almost impatiently.

She flung away from. 'If you touch me again, I shall be sick!' she told him.

Ruy stopped dead. For a moment the expression on his face was pure disbelief. Then, as if he remembered something, his eyes grew cynical and he shrugged, half turning from her.

'I'll order the car.'

And, when Pedro came to the door and knocked quietly, he didn't accompany her out or even turn from his contemplation of the darkened garden to say goodbye.

In the office, Barbara realised with a jump that she had tears on her face. She scrubbed them away angrily, gulping at the cooling coffee.

Well, at least it was over now. She might be back again in prison, as Ruy had accused her, the prison of a limited job and a narrow personal life, but at least she was safe from the volcano that was the Marquês Nieves dos Santos. After last night he would never want to see her again.

She went home late. She told herself that it was to avoid the rush hour on the London Underground, but in fact it was because she did not want to sit in her empty flat, remembering. At least at the office there was something she could do, if it was only to wash up the coffee percolator.

She sat on the train home engulfed in misery. She might have been wearing a space suit, she felt so insulated from the people around her. Even the rattle of the rapid trains seemed more muted than normal.

She was quite unaware of the curious looks she got from the travellers opposite. She did not realise that with her set face and huge, tragic eyes she looked as if she were going to her execution. It made them uncomfortable.

Home at last, she went wearily up the four flights to her flat. It was a small one, not much more than a bedsitter, right at the top of an old house. Originally it had been an artist's studio, and half the roof as well as most of one wall were made of glass. It was cold and horridly expensive to heat in the winter, but now it was filled with the light and warmth of the evening sun.

Barbara kicked off her shoes and sank down on to the single bed she used as a couch, tipping her head back into the path of a sunbeam. Slowly she allowed the tensions of the day to ooze out of her. She lifted her hand to push her hair off her brow.

Behind her a soft voice said, 'Beautiful.'

Barbara gasped. She tried to swing round and fell off the couch in a panic-stricken heap. From her undignified crouch her eyes found his figure. He was standing very still, a black shadow against that blazing window. Out of the sunlight a thin spiral of smoke wafted. Then she caught the smell, too late to act as a warning, suddenly and startlingly familiar. It had been familiar last night, in spite of the decade since she had last had it in her nostrils: the scent of a thin cigar, pungent and woody and quite unlike any other cigar she had ever encountered. Ruy's study had had that scent clinging permanently to its curtains and cushions. And, when he smoked in the evening after dinner, it stayed on his jacket, his shirt...

Barbara shut her eyes.

'What are you doing here?' she said in a whisper.

There was a pause. Then he said drily, 'Wouldn't you say we have unfinished business?'

She could not have controlled her little shudder if she had wanted to. She clasped her arms across herself, clinging on to her own shoulders for support.

'How did you get in? How did you know where...?'

The Marquês gave a soft laugh. 'Why do you think I sent you home in my car last night? Pedro told me where you lived.'

'*Why?*'

He strolled out of the shadows. 'I wanted to see where you lived. How you lived.'

She swallowed. 'I don't understand.'

Their eyes met. His were very green, like a hunting cat's. 'Don't you?'

The shivery feeling started again. She shook her head violently.

His voice took on a hard note. 'I wanted to see whether you lived alone.'

'Is that your justification for this—invasion?' she asked bitterly.

His eyes narrowed. 'Invasion? Is that what you feel? By me?'

She gave an unamused laugh and rose, spreading her hands. 'How would you feel? Your home broken into? Your privacy violated?'

Sounding bored and very cool, he said, 'How dramatic! You always were, I suppose. I merely wished to assure myself that you were unencumbered.'

Barbara did not want to pursue that. She brushed it aside, as though she were not trembling deeply, and demanded between her teeth, 'And frighten me half out of my wits?'

She sank bonelessly on to the couch. Ruy did come up to her then. He took hold of her right hand, lifted it and turned it over as if inspecting it for evidence.

'You're not frightened,' he said with superb assurance.

She clenched her teeth. 'No?'

He glanced up quickly, holding her eyes as if he were trying to draw her innermost thoughts out of her into his own brain.

'Or not of me,' he said softly.

She tore her hand away, turning a shoulder against that too-piercing regard.

'Oh, no. I'm ecstatic about being burgled by rich men who ought to know better,' she snapped, her voice oddly breathless. 'How did you get in? The lock wasn't broken.'

He shrugged. 'It's very old. I'm afraid the credit card trick worked.' He frowned at her. 'It was not at all safe.'

'I'd noticed,' said Barbara with irony.

He grinned at that suddenly, acknowledging a hit. His laughter was infectious. Barbara felt a smile tugging at her own lips—she recognised it with a sinking heart.

It was possible, she thought savagely, that the worst thing about Ruy Nieves dos Santos was that disarming laughter. When he held her, she could—just—remember that there was another lady who was his real love. But, when he laughed with that rueful amusement, he was irresistible. It was not fair, she thought, averting her eyes and trying to ignore the charm. It was like a physical quality, warm as sunshine.

'You have a right to be angry,' he acknowledged with a chuckle which confirmed all her worst fears as she felt herself begin to smile. 'Will you forgive me?'

Oh well, there was no point in holding out against the inevitable. Barbara sighed.

'You're here now. I'll put up a portcullis and drawbridge tomorrow.'

Ruy laughed. She gestured at the only chair in the room, a pine rocker.

'Sit down and tell me why you turned burglar.'

He sank into it gracefully and began to rock it backwards and forwards with an expression of innocent pleasure. Barbara's eyes narrowed. She did not trust him when he looked innocent.

But at last he said carefully and without apparent guile, 'It's Felicia, really.'

'The Marquesa?' She was startled. 'Your grandmother? What about her?'

'She's ill—very ill.' He hesitated. 'She's over here at the moment receiving treatment in the Hamilton Clinic.'

Barbara remembered that Pepita had told her much the same thing. She said sincerely, 'I'm very sorry.' The Marquesa had been a good friend ten years ago.

Still rocking, Ruy said almost idly. 'She would very much like to see you.'

'See *me*?'

He looked faintly annoyed. 'Why not? She was— is—very fond of you.'

'But it's been so long. And——' she flushed, 'Harry and I didn't exactly leave the best of reputations behind us in Portugal.'

'I wish,' he said evenly, 'you'd stop coupling yourself with your uncle. You're not responsible for the fact that he lives on his wits. And ten years ago, you were a child and hardly responsible for yourself, let alone him.'

Barbara's eyes shadowed. He would not say that if he knew that, as Harry had described it, it was her own father who had reduced her uncle to penury with his get-rich-quick schemes. The Marquês had a rigid code of honour and honesty, no matter what it cost. He would not like the paltering and the fudging of the truth which seemed to be a family trait of the Lambs.

He made an impatient sound.

She said quickly, 'Of course I'll come if she wants to see me.' Her smile was sad. 'She was always very kind to me.'

The green eyes narrowed. 'And I wasn't?'

She was startled out her memories. 'What? Oh— no... I mean...'

'I think it's fairly clear what you mean. Felicia is your friend. I am not,' he bit out.

She gave a little laugh, which broke. A *friend*? After last night—let alone what happened ten years ago when he had taken her to the edge of ecstasy and then called her a blackmailer, a cheap little blackmailer—he thought she could think of him as a friend?

The beautiful mouth compressed into a thin line until it was not beautiful at all.

He said harshly, 'I'll pick you up at your office tomorrow at noon. Be there.'

And walked out.

The next day Barbara was waiting for him. She had been waiting for over an hour, her tension increasing by the minute. Trevor, perversely, had not moved from his desk all morning, and she knew that he would take the opportunity to be unpleasant about her seeing personal friends in the office. She prayed that he would not do it to or in front of the Marquês.

In vain.

He was in the main reception area when the Marquês arrived. Barbara, for all that she was on tenterhooks, did not realise that he was there until Trevor marched back into their own office, banging angrily through the door which swung wide again with the force of his push.

'Some Scarface to see you today, my angel. Have you started running with the Mafia these days?' he snarled at her.

Barbara leaped to her feet. Behind Trevor's furious figure she could see the Marquês. It was evident from the rigid set of his features that he had heard.

'Shut up, Trevor!' she hissed.

But it was too late. The Marquês was there, looking round the office with cool eyes. She suddenly realised, looking at it from his perspective, how shoddy the small room was. The bright modern furniture and clear primary colours looked glaring. Trevor must have had the same reaction, even though he did not know the airy elegance of the South Kensington house, because he turned like an animal protecting its den.

He fixed his eyes on the livid scar.

'You ought to be more careful who you invite into the office, Barbara,' he said, not looking at her. 'I don't want it thought that we do business with the Mob's hitmen.'

As an insult it was childish and ridiculous, but it was meant to hurt. Barbara, for some reason that she could not understand, could not bear it. She did not look at the Marquês, self-possessed and cool in his perfectly tailored suit and international poise. She looked at Trevor and hated him.

'With a man like you in charge,' she said very quietly, 'It's surprising we do business at all.'

Trevor was utterly taken aback. Even the Marquês looked startled at the swiftness of the retaliation.

Barbara picked up her bag, turning her back on the silenced Trevor. Lifting her chin, she said, 'Shall we go?'

A vagrant amusement appeared in the green eyes. He held the door open for her with exaggerated ceremony. 'Whatever you say.'

She swept through the office, head high. She saw the covert glances, not at her but at his damaged face, and her heart curled up into a tight knot of pain for him. She had not forgotten how he had told her his nephew flinched from the sight; how he had been philosophical about it.

Now, for the first time, she appreciated what it must be like for him. In the Algarve, where he was known and respected, nobody remembered his disfigurement any more. She had stopped noticing it herself, all those years ago. He had that arrogance that obliterated any reaction to his scar.

But here in London, off his own ground, it was different. Seeing the curious glances in the street, the ill-disguised fascination of the girl in the office, Barbara was sharply aware how different it must be for Ruy. He was a proud man: he would hate the stares—and the pity.

The chauffeur-driven car was waiting, though today it was not Pedro at the wheel. Ruy helped her in, the scar catching the light as he bent forward. Barbara winced, averting her eyes. She at least would not add to his burden.

He did not refer to Trevor's rudeness or to her own surprising counter-attack. Instead he spoke quietly about his grandmother.

'She is very tired, but she is looking forward to seeing you. I will leave you with her. I—have many things to do.'

'Yes, of course,' murmured Barbara, still constrained by that unexpected rush of feeling.

The clinic was a pleasant place, more like a luxury hotel than a hospital. They clearly knew the Marquês. They smiled at him as he swept past the reception desk, making straight for the lift. And they did not stare at his face.

On the eleventh floor he said, 'I'll just go in and make sure the doctors aren't with her.'

Barbara nodded and he went through one of the elegant wooden-panelled doors. She wandered about the corridor, noting the elegant decoration, a positively ecclesiastical flower arrangement in the alcove opposite the lift. Then suddenly she realised that the door to the Marquesa's room had not been quite closed. Voices drifted out to her.

Gentle tones which she recognised were speaking in Portuguese. '... big risk,' the Marquesa said.

She could not hear the reply.

'There is always something to lose,' the Marquesa said, as if it were a rebuke for something her companion had said.

Another inaudible response. Then silence. Barbara was turning away when the other voice that she knew, and knew deep in her body, not just with her mind, transfixed her, saying harshly, 'What other choice do I have? There's nothing else left.'

He sounded as if he were under torture. She looked down and found her hands were clasped so tightly together that the blood had left her fingers.

I can't bear him to be hurt, she thought on a moment of discovery that alarmed her. What on earth did she mean? Why was she thinking this way?

What did Ruy Nieves dos Santos mean to her? He would be away from London and out of her life in the near future. It did not matter to her whether he was hurt or not. It could not be allowed to matter.

The Marquesa's door opened and Ruy stood there. Something of what Barbara was feeling must have shown on her face, in the wide, startled hazel eyes, the vulnerable mouth. He took an impatient step forward and immediately curbed the movement, looking at her searchingly.

Barbara, despite her discovery and her shock at it, managed a smile. She did not know how tremulous it was. His scarred mouth tightened.

'My grandmother's alone,' he said. 'Would you like to come in?'

The Marquesa looked tired. Her dark eyes seemed more sunken than Barbara remembered. One thin hand lay on the bedclothes as if she did not have the strength to lift it, but her smile at her visitor had all the old warmth.

'My dear, how kind of you to come and see me!' She looked at her grandson, an odd, admonitory look. 'Ruy, will you pour us coffee? It is in the thermos jug on the table. Now, child, come and sit by me and tell me all you've been doing.'

Barbara did her best to comply. It was not difficult. The Marquesa had always been easy to talk to, with her kindness and her unfeigned interest. Only Ruy's presence in the background introduced a new tension.

At last the Marquesa seemed to feel it, and changed the subject.

'Ruy tells me he took you to the Waterhouse. Did you enjoy it?'

Barbara flushed, partly because she was startled, partly in a rush of shame and regret. The Marquesa watched the colour flood into her visitor's pale cheeks. Her expression was thoughtful.

Barbara ignored the eagle presence behind her. 'It was very pretty,' she said woodenly.

'Yes, Dick and Alanna have made it very attractive,' the Marquesa agreed absently, her glance going from Barbara to her glowering grandson. 'You would remember them, of course. Did you see them?'

'They were away,' Ruy interjected swiftly.

Barbara flinched. Would it have made any difference if his friends had been there? Would he have been ashamed to stay the night with her if he had known himself observed by people whose opinion he cared about? Was it *because* they were away that he had allowed himself to succumb to the temptation of the moment?

'There will be other opportunities,' said the Marquesa comfortably. Her face saddened. 'Especially if Ruy is in London for a long time.'

He said strongly, 'I have promised. I'll get you home.'

The Marquesa smiled, though her eyes were wet. 'Oh, you,' she teased him, her affection evident. 'You think you're invincible! Such arrogance!'

'Arrogance? Nonsense,' he retorted, unimpressed. 'It's just a matter of planning. I am,' he added with a flash of that disarming laughter, 'good at planning.'

His grandmother shook her head at him in mock reproof. 'Sometimes I think you're too big for your boots,' she informed him. 'You don't run the world, you know.'

He came swiftly across to the bed and dropped a kiss on her cheek.

'I don't need to. Just my corner of it,' he said mischievously. 'I must be off. I'll see you later.' And in case Barbara, silent on her chair, misunderstood, he added with pointed deliberation, 'Both of you.'

CHAPTER FIVE

WHEN he was gone, Barbara felt herself relax as if someone had physically released her bonds. The Marquesa, too, seemed more at ease.

She said, 'Sometimes I worry about him, you know. He thinks it is up to him to put everything right that's wrong with the world. And this time...'

'This time?' prompted Barbara.

But the Marquesa shook her head. 'It is pointless to discuss it, and very boring. Tell me about yourself, my dear. It has been so long! We were worried, you know, when you disappeared like that. Ruy thought your uncle might have kidnapped you. He was concerned. But then we found you had taken a flight back to London, so we knew that your uncle was in the clear.' She hesitated. 'Why did you not get in touch with us again?'

Barbara looked down at her clasped hands. This was the point at which she could burst out with accusations against the Marquesa's adored grandson. She had dreamed about it, to begin with, when she was still hurt and burning to hurt him in return. Now it seemed pointless and unkind to the old lady in front of her. So she said evasively, 'I wanted to put everything behind me and start again.'

The Marquesa nodded, but her eyes were puzzled. The Marquesa had never had to face a hopeless situation in the whole of her well-ordered life. She had certainly never run away.

'It was I who found you, you know,' she said with a smile. 'A friend of mine in Puerto Banus was approached by your firm. I saw your name on the notepaper.'

Oh lord, the Marquesa must be the elderly lady Trevor was proposing to cheat! Barbara paled. The old lady did not notice.

'I even wrote to you, but then Pepita said she would go to your office herself.'

So they talked—a little—about Pepita.

'It is a shame,' said the Marquesa, looking at Barbara keenly. 'They were not ideally suited, of course, but then which of us is? And they had much in common.'

'I suppose so,' murmured Barbara, acutely uncomfortable.

'Ruy was very—upset,' his grandmother said.

She could have laughed. If Ruy was in love, he must have been a great deal more than upset: devastated, angry, betrayed, reckless. Reckless enough to take another, unimportant, lady to bed as consolation?

'Upsetting those plans of his,' his grandmother went on, unaware of Barbara's inner reflections.

'Plans?' Barbara looked up.

The Marquesa sighed. 'I was supposed to be going back to the *quinta* after the wedding,' she said simply. 'I thought it was a mistake, myself. Young people should be on their own when they are first married. But Ruy laughed, and you know what he's like.'

Was that why Pepita had cried off? Because of the responsibility of caring for his grandmother in the house which the old lady was used to running? Barbara wondered. Pepita had not said so but, even at the time, she had had the feeling that there was something that Pepita was holding back.

'I never thought Ruy would marry,' the Marquesa was saying matter-of-factly.

Barbara stared. 'Why on earth...?'

'He doesn't like people getting close to him. And of course there is that scar. Not every woman would like it.'

'That's ridiculous,' said Barbara hotly. 'He's a very attractive man! I wish everyone would stop talking about him as if he's some sort of monster.'

The Marquesa gave a small, private smile, as if she had won a victory in a game that Barbara did not even know they had been playing. She looked at the older woman suspiciously.

'You're quite right,' the Marquesa said comfortably. 'Absolutely. I keep hoping that he will meet somebody who will make him believe it.'

And after that she changed the subject again, decisively.

As Barbara was standing up to go, the Marquesa in a sudden unexpected gesture stretched up to kiss her on both cheeks. 'You're a good child,' she said. 'I wish Luis...'

Barbara looked down at the tired face. 'The boy?'

The Marquesa sighed. 'Fernando's son. He is not easy. He needs a mother, of course. Ruy is so prickly with him, sometimes too stern, sometimes crazily indulgent. I ought to do something about it, but I have been so tired. I was remembering what you were like. You were not so much older than Luis back then, and in just as big a muddle.' She sighed again. 'I wish he had someone like you to talk to,' she said. 'Ruy and I are too removed. Fantasy,' she said, dismissing it with a sudden return to briskness. 'But it was good to see you again, my dear. Come again soon.' She bit her lip. 'I'll be here for a long time.'

Barbara's heart turned over with pity. She touched the frail hand reassuringly. 'I'll come,' she promised.

Outside, she half expected the Marquês to be waiting for her, but the tree-lined street was empty of all but parked cars. She walked slowly in the direction of a Tube station. Trevor would be angry, she thought. She did not really care. It was time she left Trevor's employment.

For weeks she had been uneasy about his style of business, but now it was different. After that cruel insult to Ruy this morning, she felt she could not bear to see Trevor again. She no longer had to work herself up to take the decision. In that single spiteful moment this morning, Trevor had made it impossible for her to continue working for him.

It was, she thought ruefully, rather a relief. Though getting a new job would not be easy. And, after Harry's last descent on London, she had no savings to speak of to see her through a difficult patch. Still, there was no point in putting it off, since her mind was made up. She stopped in at a couple of agencies on the way back to the office and put her name down on their books.

* * *

The Marquês was waiting for her when she left work that night. He came up to her as she was locking the door behind her. Barbara closed her eyes briefly as he touched her on the arm. Deep down, she was not even surprised.

'Can I give you a lift?' he murmured, his tone full of suppressed laughter.

Barbara sighed. 'You're going home by way of Baron's Court?'

'You,' he told her, taking the keys and her briefcase from her, 'are going home via Kensington. I have a bottle of champagne on ice. No working girl could resist it.'

She shook her head, but she was laughing. 'You're probably right,' she said resignedly. 'All right, I'll come quietly.'

He was driving himself. And when they arrived at the tall white house it seemed deserted. Their footsteps echoed oddly as he turned the key and ushered her into the hallway.

'In here,' said Ruy abruptly.

He was suddenly less urbane, less amused. She thought he was looking her over as if he were sizing her up as an opponent. His face was grave.

The room he indicated was a small sitting-room. There were a couple of chairs, an enormous desk and books everywhere. Except for the light streaming in through the sash windows, and the cheerful autumnal chintz, it was a replica of his study in the *quinta*. Smaller, of course, and not so magnificent. There was no eighteenth-century globe here, no dark oil paintings on brocade-hung walls. But the untidiness was the same, the untidiness and the sense of a strong personality pursuing its own obsessions. Instinctively Barbara's muscles tightened.

Ruy made a gesture at one of the chairs, but she ignored it. He shrugged, then went to perch on the corner of his crowded desk and looked down at his hands.

'I won't keep you long,' he said formally. 'It isn't a lengthy process, I understand.'

Barbara stared at him, trying to quell her foreboding. 'What isn't?'

His eyes lifted swiftly and fell again to the study of the fingers clasped loosely about one raised knee.

'Proposing marriage,' he said coolly.

She gasped.

Into the silence he murmured, 'You were expecting something different?'

He knew quite well what she had been expecting, Barbara thought, colouring furiously. Moreover, after his disgraceful behaviour that terrible night, she had every justification for expecting it. She drew a deep breath.

Ruy shifted. 'I wish you'd stop standing there looking like St Joan,' he complained. 'It puts me off.'

She glared at him. 'Good!'

He shook his head, managing to look hurt.

'Don't be unkind,' he said reproachfully. 'You don't know how nerve-racking it is.'

Barbara snorted. He might scare her witless, with his power and his detestable charm, but she was not going to put up with this sort of thing.

'You look it,' she said drily.

Suddenly Ruy gave one of his disarming laughs. He held out a hand to her.

'Well, I might. You're very intimidating, do you know that?'

'I can see that you're shaking in your shoes,' Barbara said, avoiding that horribly inviting hand by sitting down. She met his eyes levelly. 'What on earth do you mean by it?'

He stopped smiling. For a moment his eyes were veiled, then he sighed. He was not play-acting now, she realised with a flash of perception. This was not a predator toying with his captured prey, this was a desperately worried man. She doubted whether he was even aware of her identity, except incidentally. He might have been talking to anyone; he was really talking to himself.

'Felicia's getting worse. She looks exhausted all the time. And she's so unhappy. Worried about the brat, worried about dying in a strange country. He ran a hand through his dark hair. It did not look as if it were the first time he had done so today. He looked crumpled, preoccupied and so tired that, notwithstanding her case against him, Barbara's heart went out to her embattled enemy.

'I spoke to Archer this morning—he's her consultant. He says she ought to do what she wants and go home. But——' he smashed one fist into his open palm with a sudden fury that made Barbara jump, 'there has to be someone to run the place. Run the boy.'

'Pepita...' said Barbara.

'Pepita's made her decision,' Ruy said swiftly. 'I don't deny I was—disappointed, but there's no going back.'

'And you need a wife now,' Barbara finished for him.

'I——' He hesitated. 'Yes,' he said at last, watching her.

She looked away, conscious of his eyes on her, unaware of her own air of painful tension.

He said her name very softly, as if it were shaken out of him. She thought he had made a move towards her and half turned, bracing herself. But he was still sitting in that negligent pose, only a slight tension in the clasped fingers revealing his mood. He met her eyes gravely.

She shook her head, her confusion and indecision evident. It had never occurred to her that he might want to marry her. Of course, she corrected herself, he did not *want* to marry her. But it was extraordinary enough that he would think her suitable even for an alliance of convenience like this. He knew all about her background, her undesirable relations, her slightly dubious present employer. He knew that she did not know how to run a large household like that at the *quinta*, that she had no idea how to dress beautifully, entertain graciously, instruct servants. Or, God help her, bring up a difficult pre-adolescent.

He knew all of that. He must know too, or at least guess, that the prospect would terrify her. And she would probably do it badly.

'It won't be much comfort to the Marquesa if I run her house into the ground,' she remarked. 'Has it occurred to you that I might add to her anxieties rather than relieve her of them?'

Ruy sat very still. 'It's possible,' he allowed at last.

It was very likely, thought Barbara in despair. Why, oh, why did she want to do it? She had none of the right training and all the wrong instincts. She knew that. But the sudden vision of herself married to Ruy had a startling effect, as if she were looking at a picture that she had seen years ago and now recognised again. It was uncanny. Fighting herself more than him, she said desperately, 'I've never had to look after anyone but myself.'

'But you've had to do rather too much of that.'

It was an odd remark and she stopped, her whirling thoughts arrested by that soft-voiced statement. He was looking at her, the cruel scar very pronounced.

'I would, of course, look after you,' Ruy told her. It was like a vow.

It moved her, but it also brought back her earlier trepidation. She shifted, biting her lip.

He expelled a long breath. 'Well, at least you're thinking,' he said at last, in a voice so like his normal ironic tones that she almost jumped. 'What can I say to aid the process?'

'You've already said more than enough,' Barbara told him drily.

'I have,' Ruy agreed with angry self-mockery.

For a moment she did not understand him. Then she felt the colour rush painfully into her face and hated it. What a fool he must think her!

With difficulty she said, 'I—am very fond of the Marquesa. I—do sympathise, honestly. I'd like to help. If only...'

He looked at her steadily, not helping.

'Isn't there another way?' she asked miserably. 'Couldn't I be—oh, a housekeeper or something?'

He said with suppressed violence, 'Don't you see, you stupid girl, I need someone to take the *responsibility*? Not to do the day-to-day work. But to be the—oh, the mistress of the household, if you like.'

Barbara swallowed. 'In that case, why did you try to make me your mistress?' she said, almost inaudibly.

There was a long, long silence. She could not look at him.

Then he said slowly, 'It did not seem to me that the two were exactly incompatible.'

She stared at him in disbelief then. He was frowning, the muscle in the scarred cheek working. When he spoke again, it seemed that he was choosing his words with care.

'Is that your major objection?'

Barbara's throat was dry. She had never been so embarrassed in her life, nor felt so vulnerable. She swallowed.

Ruy did not lay a hand on her. Her skin felt icy. She felt as if that still, brooding presence had thrown a net round her. Yet nobody spoke in that still, sunlit room.

At last she said, 'If...I couldn't...I don't want...'

'To go to bed with me?' he finished gravely. 'Yes, I realise that.'

Her eyes flew to his, wide and half ashamed.

'You made it very clear,' he reminded her. 'I hoped that...'

'What?' she asked as he in his turn broke off.

'You're alone in the world,' he said at length, surprising her again, 'and you're an affectionate creature. What about children?'

She stared at him.

'Marriage is for life,' he reminded her. 'Can you give up any prospect of children?'

Barbara said, 'I've seen enough of what can happen to children. I'm not doing that to anyone else.'

If anything, his frown deepened. 'Are you sure? Never?'

She shook her head forcefully.

'I wish I could be sure...'

'You can,' she assured him. 'I don't want children and I'm not likely to change my mind about it. That's not an obstacle.'

Ruy looked at her doubtfully. Then he said, 'Does that mean that you will marry me?'

Barbara jumped. She had not realised, but at some point in the conversation she had surrendered her objections. It was madness and she knew it. But when she saw him look like that, grey and worn down, as if all his splendid arrogance were no longer enough, she could not help herself.

Sensing her hesitation, he said rapidly, 'I need you, Barbara.'

She gave a long sigh, part despair, part relief that the battle was over.

'I'll marry you,' she said.

*　　*　　*

One of the things she had to do was tell Pepita. She had not spoken to her friend since she had telephoned to report her safe delivery of the betrothal ring. She did not know how Pepita would take this piece of news. At the very least, it was not flattering that the Marquês had transferred his affections so quickly.

But Pepita seemed unperturbed. She looked at Barbara searchingly.

'Is this what you want?' Ruy can be very—forceful. Has he bullied you?'

'No,' said Barbara truthfully.

'Well, you don't look very happy,' Pepita informed her. 'You'll have to do better than that for the photographers, or you'll get him in the gossip magazines as a wife-beater.'

Ruy himself said much the same thing.

'Do you think,' he said one evening, a slight edge to his pleasant voice, 'that you could manage to look a little more bridal?'

They were about to go out, standing on the steps of the Kensington house waiting for Pedro to bring the car. Barbara was wearing one of the new dresses Ruy had insisted on, a shimmer of green that skimmed her slender hips, swirling out below the knee to reveal sheer stockings and heels higher than anything she had ever worn in her life before. She was wearing her hair off her face and clipped with emeralds to match the emeralds at her throat and on her wrist. She looked expensive and tasteful but, as he said, she did not look happy.

She said brightly, 'It's very bridal to look nervous.'

He frowned. 'Nerouvs, maybe, not scared to death. Do you think you could at least pretend you want to marry me for the duration of the evening?'

The words hurt, and Barbara whitened. But she suffered his arm round her bare shoulders as they went into the big hotel where they were to meet Dick and Alanna and the rest of their party.

It was some sort of charity dance. Barbara had hardly taken in the object of the fund-raising. She was learning to cope with the formality, and the crowds of fashionably dressed people who all knew the Marquês, but she had not yet learned to tell one from the other.

They ate at the top table; Ruy was clearly some sort of guest of honour. Barbara herself received as many curious looks as compliments, and was the target of a number of photographers. Eventually Ruy took her to dance, his hand burning between her naked shoulderblades. Every flashlight in the hall, it seemed to her, clicked at them.

On the sprung floor he took her into his arms easily, as if there were no memories to be suppressed of her having been there before. Barbara caught her breath, and he looked down at her.

'Don't take any notice of them. They'll grow tired of us quickly enough once we're safely married.'

She shook her head, the emeralds glinting. 'It's not that. I just hate . . .'

'The photographs won't be pretty,' he said sardonically, as if he were agreeing with something she said, 'but you don't have to look at them.'

It was as if he meant to hurt her. She felt tears spring to her eyes and was too proud to let him see them. She turned her head away so he could only see her profile, saying, 'You don't make it any easier for me.'

He gave a harsh laugh. 'What could, my delicate wife-to-be? Plastic surgery?'

She winced then, unable to prevent herself. 'Don't,' she said involuntarily.

But the lights lowered then and the tempo of the music changed and, like every other man on the dance-floor, Ruy gathered his partner closer. It was extraordinary how, even surrounded by a hundred other swaying couples, she felt as if they were alone when his body enfolded hers like this. Alone and on the brink of something that spelt the end of her peace of mind for ever.

She gave a sigh of relief when the dance ended. Ruy gave her one mocking look as they left the floor. He surrendered her at once to Dick, who took her back to the music and jived energetically while he told her how glad he and Alanna were about the marriage. He did not say that he was astounded by his friend's choice of bride. He did not, thought Barbara wryly, have to.

And it was not just Ruy's friends.

'Why does he want you?' Dan Leonard said, frowning. 'What's he up to?'

Introduced by Barbara, he and the Marquês had treated each other with the careful courtesy of opposing battle commanders.

She could not answer him, of course, so she shrugged.

'He's not trying to make you pay some sort of debt, is he?' Dan went on uneasily.

Barbara stared at him.

'That property in Puerto Banus—the old girl's solicitor wrote to Trevor, you know. And she's some sort of Marquesa. A relative?'

Barbara's heart sank. She remembered the Marquesa's words. 'A friend.'

'Well, somebody wrote to us. And Trevor took the letter and I've not seen it since. It wasn't typed.'

Memory flickered and became a clear picture. The handwritten letter. It must have been the letter that the Marquesa had written to her which she had never received, though why Trevor had suppressed it she could not guess. She told Dan.

'Spite,' he said with confidence. 'Also guilty conscience.' He hesitated. 'I've told him that if he goes ahead with that scheme, I'm leaving. I think I've scotched it. He can't afford to lose both of us.'

'Thank you,' said Barbara with relief. 'I didn't dare hope for a happy ending.'

Dan gave her a crooked smile. 'I just wish I thought you'd got one yourself. You'd come back if you were ever in trouble, wouldn't you? To us, I mean. To your friends.' He paused and then added in a rush, 'I just don't like the way he looks at you sometimes.'

But Ruy was always courtesy itself, in private as in public. He made her accompany him a good deal in those weeks before their marriage. They went to receptions and cocktail parties and private views, as if, as she told him drily, they were some sort of minor royalty.

Ruy shrugged. 'Saturation publicity.'

'What do you mean?' It was after a particularly long evening at a particularly crowded art gallery. Barbara had come home with him and kicked off her shoes before subsiding on to the velvet sofa. Later, whenever she asked him to, he would take her home. In private, by contrast to their public engagements, he never once touched her.

He gave her a crooked smile. 'If we go out and about devotedly now, they'll lose interest. Then we can have all our rows in decent privacy.'

Barbara slowly rotated her tired ankles. The fashionable shoes on which Alanna and Pepita were united in purchasing for her were more elegant than comfortable. It amused Ruy, which was just as well. It made a talking point.

'Rows?' she echoed now, rubbing her calves.

He watched her lazily. 'Most married couples fight from time to time.'

The thought alarmed her, though she did her best to disguise the fact. 'I hope we shan't.'

'We're not *that* unusual,' he added drily. 'I'm no saint, and neither are you. I imagine a row or two will be inevitable.'

She lifted her head. 'I don't want a battle, Ruy. I—I couldn't handle it.'

The amusement drained out of his face, leaving it strained and tired. The scar stood out tonight. As if he sensed her looking at it, he shifted suddenly, turning his unmarked profile towards her. 'OK,' he said lightly, 'no battle. Along with all the other things you—can't handle.'

Barbara sat up on the sofa, her face disturbed. It was the first time that Ruy had suggested that her conditions bothered him. For a moment she felt a flicker of hope that he might, after all, care for her a little. Not as much as for Pepita, perhaps, but a little. But then she looked at the lazily drooping lids and the ironic mask of a face, and she knew that all he was talking about was the conventions. He did not have to love a lady to take her to bed, as he had already demonstrated beyond any doubt, and he was faintly impatient with her failure to share his own attitude.

She fell back among the cushions, disappointed. Ruy stood up.

'Added to those, I think, must be private views.' He sat down on the sofa and began to massage her feet with strong, steady movements. 'I thought I was going to have to carry you out of there this evening.'

'Now that,' said Barbara, grateful for this return to the superficialities on which their relationship was going to have to survive, 'would have been a picture and a half!'

He looked down at her ankles, his smile wry. 'Beauty and the Beast, you feel?'

She could not bear this denigration of his appearance. It was almost as if he wanted to hurt himself, to keep pressing on the wound. It hurt her almost more than she could bear to see him do it, and she had no idea how to handle her own pain or his. But she said steadily, 'I'm a bride, not a beast, and I'll thank you to remember it.'

His eyes lifted and he was laughing. Almost, for a split second, it seemed as if he was going to lean forward and touch that smiling mouth to her own. She felt her muscles clench in anticipation.

And then he was standing, striding to the un-curtained window, throwing lightly over his shoulder, 'A hobbling bride. If you don't get yourself some shoes you can walk in, I'll cancel the wedding.'

And after that they laughed and chatted, and later, scrupulously not touching so much as the sleeve of her dress, he drove her home.

They were married, eventually, in a simple register office ceremony that the Press failed to get wind of. Barbara wore a tailored ivory suit and pearls which Ruy gave her the night before with a quaint little bow. The Marquesa was released from the hospital to attend, but Ruy's nephew Luis was not recalled from France. Dick and Alanna were wit-nesses. She'd thought of inviting Dan Leonard, but he was out of town. They all had a celebration lunch in the restaurant of a famous hotel before Ruy and Barbara left for the *quinta*.

To Barbara it all seemed faintly unreal. The ar-rangements went like clockwork, but somehow none of it seemed important enough. It might have been any appointment, any delicious lunch with friends. It was none of it as significant as she had somehow expected.

Dick and Alanna were the perfect companions, friendly and discreet.

'I suppose you'll have a big party when Felicia's better,' Alanna said.

'How traditional you are, Alanna!' drawled Ruy, after a moment.

She looked startled. 'Well, won't you? I mean, won't people expect...?'

He shrugged. 'We'll do whatever Barbara wants. I don't intend to entertain to fulfil people's expectations, but to give my wife pleasure.'

Dick and Alanna beamed. It sounded perfect, of course, Barbara thought cynically. Odd, then, that it should make her feel so desolate. For if she had been Pepita he would have meant it, smiling across the table at her for more than form's sake. She smiled, but it was with an effort. The green eyes narrowed. But this was not a private occasion and they were to some extent on display: Ruy did not demand an explanation.

But later, on the way to the airport, he said softly, 'What is it?'

She turned away. He was too perceptive. 'Nothing.'

'My dear girl, I have eyes,' he said drily. 'Do you think that because you won't look at me, I can't see you either? Something was wrong back there. I want to know what.'

She sighed. 'If you must know—it will sound silly—but it didn't seem quite real. It frightened me, just for a minute. It was all so easy. And—and neat.' She gulped. 'Only—not real.'

For a long minute there was silence, then Ruy said with deep irony, 'Well, it wouldn't, would it?'

Her eyes flew to his, startled. For a moment she was on the brink of replying hotly, 'It would if I were Pepita,' but she held it down, forced it down.

The marriage was only going to work if she did not keep thinking about Pepita and remembering that this was not what he really wanted. So she quelled her sudden fury of rebellion, and her eyes fell.

'No,' she said quietly, 'I suppose not.'

CHAPTER SIX

IT WAS very still. In the distance, miles away across the valley, there was the sound of some machine, perhaps an electric saw, but here all was silence.

Barbara turned luxuriously as she drifted into wakefulness. Through the open window the sun streamed, bringing with it the scent of lemon trees and the sea. For a moment she lay in drowsy peace. Then she opened her eyes. Above her the filmy hangings of the four-poster were wafting gently in the breeze off the sea. She put up an idle hand to touch them, reflecting wryly that her first waking thought at home would have been to look at her watch. She stretched, then got out of bed.

The room was simple but deeply luxurious, with its marquetry-inlaid cupboards and Louis Quinze chairs. Barbara looked at her clothes, flung away carelessly last night across one of those precious antiques. The contrast with her former life could not have been greater.

She padded across to the window and leaned on the sill, letting the warm wind from the sea riffle her hair. The prospect before her was almost tropical, with its palms and bougainvillaea of burning magenta. The air smelt spicy.

Even in London, with Pepita taking her shopping for a bank-breaking wardrobe and Ruy ruthlessly putting her on display, she had not really grasped how different her life was going to be, she thought. Most of the things that had occupied her up to now were simply no longer important. She did not have to remember small things like buying shampoo or replacing kitchen salt. All of that was done for her by Elena. She did not have to worry about loose buttons or damaged tights. The mending was done by a girl from the village, and snagged tights were simply thrown away. Money, which she had never really thought about before, had removed most of her daily concerns.

Which left her with—what? Barbara sighed, looking across the perfect landscape. Too much time, she thought ruefully. Too much time to remember, too much time to look forward and worry.

Yet here she was in a jewel of a house, free from worries, waited on hand and foot, basking in sunshine, and all she felt was a blank foreboding. *Why?* Was it this strange marriage? She had worried about it beforehand, but now it seemed as if it was working out better than she could have expected.

Ruy was a surprisingly easy partner. The staff were friendly, the workers on the estate were positively welcoming. And not one of Ruy's friends in the neighbourhood who had called on them had indicated by word or look that they remembered Barbara from her raggle-taggle days as a member of the more raffish end of the English community. Why then did she feel uneasy?

She turned back into the room. Her eye fell on the tumbled linen of the high bed, and she sighed. The answer was not so far to seek. She had expected Ruy to be remote, preoccupied, to retire to his study to work as he had done years before. She could not have been more wrong.

For one thing, he spent most of his days with her. He had plainly been away from the *quinta* for some time. Now that he was back he visited the fields, talked to the tenants and the farm manager, went round the orchards. Sometimes he walked, sometimes he rode. But, whichever he chose, he wanted Barbara with him.

She had been embarrassed at first. She could not help herself, she was still startled every time anyone addressed her as Senhora Marquesa. But nobody was hostile, as she had expected, or contemptuous, as she had been prepared for. They were all like Elena—pleased, interested, welcoming.

She remarked on it to Ruy, and he gave her that grin which was so rare and to which she never failed to respond.

'They're romantics to a man. They'd given me up. Now that I'm married, they regard it as their very own soap opera,' he said.

Barbara was puzzled. 'But Pepita...'

The grin disappeared. 'I got engaged to Pepita in Lisbon, and disengaged in London. It did not have much impact here.'

'Whereas I'm on screen daily,' said Barbara drily.

He laughed, relaxing. 'Quite. How does it feel to be a star?'

She warmed to his teasing, as she always did. 'A responsibility.'

He gave a shout of laughter and took her hand. 'Make sure you don't forget your lines, then,' he said, leaning from his own horse to kiss the tip of her nose.

Barbara was getting used to these lightning caresses, and managed not to fall off her horse, or to pull at the reins so that the poor beast reared. She did not, however, manage to keep her breathing steady or her colour even. Ruy appeared delighted with the effect. He was in bounding good spirits for the rest of the day.

Barbara began to realise that she had never really seen him happy before. In London he had been worried, preoccupied; heartbroken, she supposed, over Pepita's defection. And ten years ago he had been suspicious, his main objective to defend his grandmother from people he saw as a bunch of crooks. She had never seen him light-hearted. Nor, she realised over the days, had he ever before turned the full strength of his charm on her.

Oh, she knew that he had had a reputation for being irresistible. According to the locals, any woman was his for the price of a smile. But she had thought it was local mythology, a fantasy about the countryside's most eligible bachelor. Now she saw the myth for what it was: the unvarnished truth. Even she could have fallen victim to it, and she knew not only that he wanted Pepita rather than herself but that, in his heart of hearts, he despised her. But when he laughed at her, tipping her hat over her eyes as she rode like a naughty schoolboy, holding her tantalisingly two feet off the ground when he helped her off her horse, she could almost throw caution to the winds.

It became harder and harder to say a calm good-night to him, as the candles guttered and the stars above the terrace turned into a lacework of brilliance. Sometimes she wondered whether Ruy knew how hard it was becoming. There was something in the way he looked at her, searchingly. There was something, a faint thread of awareness, almost of mockery, in the courteous voice that wished her an undisturbed night.

When she got up to that elegant room, no matter how tired she was, she could not sleep. She told herself it was the heat, and opened windows and shutters to the sea. But still she could not sleep. She thought it was the claustrophobic hangings of the four-poster bed, or the sheer size of it, but she was unable to reason herself out of sleeplessness. In the end she took to leaving open the door on to the internal veranda, so that there was a through draught from courtyard to open countryside.

One night, when she had been lying dusty-eyed under the single sheet for what seemed like hours, that door was pushed wider. She heard it creak, and wondered briefly whether there were a breath of wind in that hot night, after all. But then she saw the shadow.

He came and stood at the end of the bed, a shadow among shadows. He said her name very softly.

It did not occur to Barbara to pretend she was asleep.

'Can't you sleep?' Ruy asked quietly, as if he was whispering in order not to waken the house, which, given how far away the servants slept, was ridiculous.

Barbara pushed her damp hair off her face. 'It's so hot,' she said.

Ruy sat down on the bed beside her and put the back of his hand against her skin. It was very cool; so cool that she felt something jump and twist inside her at the touch, as if she had had a small electric shock.

'Maybe you've been doing too much. Or in the sun more than you can take.'

Barbara shook her head. 'I've been careful. Anyway, I know how much sun I can take. This isn't the first time I've lived here, don't forget.'

'How could I?' said Ruy in an odd voice.

Barbara, who had for once not been thinking of their old battle, gasped and bit her lip, subsiding into embarrassed silence.

He sat unmoving. In the darkness he seemed both very big and yet insubstantial, as if she would put her hand through him if she reached out to touch him. Barbara began to shake. She felt as if she were on the edge of a precipice, not knowing how she got there, with no idea what to do next or even what she wanted. She held her breath.

At last he spoke in a low, troubled tone. 'You're not happy, are you? That's the real problem. You keep remembering.'

She moved sharply. Ruy turned his head, a slow movement in the darkness, and she caught the glimmer of his eyes. He was watching her.

'I see it,' he said simply. 'One moment you are enjoying yourself. Then something calls it back to your mind and—in a second—you're buttoned up again.' He leaned forward. 'Barbara, leave the past behind.'

She closed her eyes against that appeal. 'How?' she asked wearily.

'It was ten years ago, for God's sake. No matter how bad it was, no matter how unhappy, you haven't lived with your uncle for ten years. It can't still govern your life. You mustn't let it. *I* won't let it.'

It was almost funny: he thought it was her life with Harry which still left her burning with shame whenever she thought about it. Had he forgotten his part in her life, to say nothing of her departure from Portugal? Had he forgotten carrying her into the house, caring for her and then calling her a blackmailer? Had he forgotten taking her in his arms in the study? Had he forgotten the money he had thrown at her to buy her off, to get rid of her?

Ruy put out his hands and grasped her shoulders, shaking her a little.

'Answer me!'

'It's not so easy,' she said evasively.

She could feel his eyes searching her face in the darkness. 'Do you still see him?'

'Harry?' She gave a dry laugh. 'Oh yes, he turns up from time to time.' Usually when he needed money, but she did not say that to Ruy; he already knew it, and anyway, she did not want to give him any more reasons for despising her.

'Will he follow you here? Is that what you're afraid of?'

She lifted her shoulders. 'Who knows?'

'Do you think I can't protect you?' he said, suppressed rage in his voice. 'Do you think I'll let him? He won't get over the threshold—you can rely on that.'

He sounded appallingly grim. Barbara thought with a shiver that she felt sorry for her uncle if Harry ever did try to approach Ruy. She hoped devoutly that he would not. It would be the final humiliation.

She said politely, 'I'm sure I can.'

Ruy gave a little exasperated sigh. 'Then *why*...?'

She had that cold feeling of imminent danger again, and swallowed. It sounded thunderous in the dark.

Ruy said gently, 'Barbara, you can't put yourself in chains for ever.'

In a voice she did not recognise, she said, 'I don't know what you mean.'

He seemed to hesitate. Then, very slowly, he leaned towards her. Barbara held her breath. So gently that she hardly felt his fingers against her skin, he drew the back of his hand down her cheek. She gave a silent gasp as her whole body clenched. It might be the most fleeting of touches, but every atom within her responded to it, as if he were a magnet and her whole body was impelled towards him on a force-field so strong that her frightened mind could not resist.

She clutched the edge of the sheet and almost dragged herself away from him, eyes tight shut.

He said reflectively, 'Do you know, I get two distinct messages from you?'

Barbara's jaw ached with tension. 'I don't understand.'

He laughed softly, not dismayed by the wooden little voice. 'Then let me explain.' The laugh again. 'Or better still, let me show you.'

'What do you want?' she cried, pressing herself into the pillows.

'Oh, I think you know that,' he said negligently. 'It is what *you* want, or don't want, which is so interesting. For example, sometimes you pull away from me, like you're doing now. Like you did at Dick and Alanna's.'

Barbara caught her breath, but he ignored the little sound of distress.

'And sometimes you touch me, as if you want to. As if you want me to touch you. As if you want this—this ghost of a marriage to come to life.'

'No!' It was pure instinct, a cry of rejection.

'It would only be natural,' he said soothingly. 'You're young and affectionate and—attractive.' He was going to say something else, she knew. What was it? Something that revealed he had seen her hunger and pitied her for it? He was more experienced than she was, of course; he would recognise sexual compulsion sooner than she had herself. Did he think he owed her, that he had to satisfy that shameful urge?

'No,' she said under her breath, torn with humiliation at her thoughts.

'Why pretend?' Ruy sounded strained. 'Why keep trying to behave as if you're a sexless zombie? Just because you're normal, it's nothing to be ashamed of.'

Barbara twisted away from him. 'You're wrong...you don't understand...I'm not...' she said incoherently.

Ruy stayed maddeningly calm. 'As I said, let me show you.' His voice was even. His body was very controlled. He did not make any sudden or clumsy move. Barbara felt that she was being hunted by an artist. She tried to free herself from the tangled sheet, to struggle out of the bed, but he caught her easily and held her without force. She closed her eyes as his head came down to hers.

She heard him murmur again, 'Let me.'

He embraced her with his whole body. Her blood seemed to beat to the rhythm of his, her skin to quicken at the touch of his, her very heartbeat to be driven by his own. For a moment she was lost, frightened, tossed on a giant whirlpool of feeling. His kiss absorbed her and she became his creature. He seemed to breathe for her.

But then she felt the roughness of his scar against her breast, and the memory she had never quite suppressed lanced through her. Suddenly she was eighteen again, eighteen and mortally hurt. She twisted out of his arms, frantic, and off the bed.

'No!' she sobbed. 'Not again—I can't bear it!'

CHAPTER SEVEN

THE HOUSE was still. It was very early; so early that the sun was still muted and there were diamond drops of dew on the vine leaves. Elena and her husband were still sleeping. Even the dogs in the stable were still sleeping.

Barbara had never opened the french windows before. She struggled with the bolts, trying not to make a noise. Eventually she had them open. After that she had to open the decorative grille gates that covered them. They were noisier and for a moment she froze. But no sounds came from the sleeping house and she relaxed again.

She went out, past the terrace with its shading vines, past the velvet lawn, so unusual in the climate, which the gardeners watered daily. She was wearing jeans and stout shoes which rapidly turned black with the early morning damp. She walked through the orchard.

She had not slept.

After she had torn herself away from Ruy last night she had felt flayed, desperate. All she wanted was that he leave her. He saw that, of course; he was too acute not to. He was too acute to try to touch her either. But he had not gone. Instead he had turned, reclining on the bed, asking, coaxing, talking, trying to make her tell him the pictures in her head which filled her with such pain. He had not succeeded. But he had recalled the past so vividly that, even after he'd eventually left her, Barbara had tossed and turned and failed to get rid of it.

Now, at barely sunrise, she walked restlessly through the long meadow plants under his trees. It was here, she thought, here that she... No, not that she had first seen him. She had seen him first at the stable, talking to Pepita. Then she'd seen him again in Dick's bar while the detestable Brian Gallaher had had his arm round her. She had looked across the cool room and met those strange green eyes, several degrees colder than the aggressively air-conditioned bar. It had been Dick who had told her who he was. It had been Dick, too, who had warned her that Ruy was very protective of his grandmother and that he had heard and did not approve of her befriending the little English waif who helped Pepita with her riding school.

She leaned against the bark of a lemon tree, standing among its branches so that she was hidden from sight. The bark was rough to the touch but warm. The leaves had the faint tangy smell that she always recalled in her dreams. Though it had been night time, of course, when he had found her, not brilliant day with the dew on the leaves.

Barbara tipped her head back and looked up through the leaves at the powder-blue sky. Her eyes were aching with tears. That was odd, she thought. She had not cried then, or later.

It had been Harry's fault, at least to begin with. He'd been involved in a property deal with Brian Gallaher. It had reached the stage, already too

familiar to Barbara, when things were beginning to
go wrong. Harry, of course, had spent all the money
Gallaher had advanced him, and the big man
wanted payment. Harry hadn't had it. Anyway,
Harry—typically again—hadn't believed that the
project was hopeless. He'd wanted a little more
time, a little more money... Gallaher, for some
inexplicable reason, had allowed himself to be
persuaded.

Except that the reason was not inexplicable.
Probably everyone had known the reason, thought
Barbara, still humiliated by the memory; everyone
but herself.

Ten years ago she had been a leggy eighteen-year-
old. Most of the time she'd spent in T-shirts and
shorts which were slightly too small for her because
there had been no money for new clothes. Her
scrappy education had not fitted her for much and
she'd earned what she could: helping out Dick and
Alanna—who had given her a uniform when she
waitressed for them—grooming horses and oc-
casionally giving Pepita's smaller pupils careful
rides along the shore.

All the time she had been saving money to pay
her return fare to England, to seek some sort of
education, to find a career. Harry's dubious beach-
comber ways hadn't suited her. Besides, he'd had
a girlfriend living with him then, and Louise had
not liked sharing her home with an eighteen-year-
old orphan.

Barbara had often wondered if it had been
Louise's idea, rather than Harry's. In his careless
way her uncle had been fond of Barbara, and he'd

known how innocent she was. It had never occurred to him before to use her youthful attractions to pay his debts.

This time had been different, though... Harry and Louise announced that they were going to Spain looking for further partners in their property venture. Barbara was to stay behind and look after the Villa Branca which Harry was nominally caretaking. And, in case she was nervous on her own, Harry told her with suspicious nonchalance, he had arranged for his good friend Brian to come and spend a few days at the villa to keep her company.

Gallaher was a rich businessman who had just been through a traumatic divorce. He never stopped talking about his ex-wife, who he felt had cheated him. Barbara was slightly sorry for him, though she did not like the way he was always putting his arm proprietorially round her. It never occurred to her that a man so much older, and so preoccupied by another woman, would have any designs on herself.

In that she was wrong, as anyone else in the place could have told her. Or so Pepita told her afterwards.

'I thought you knew,' Pepita had said, remorseful in retrospect. 'He was so *obvious*.'

'But *why*?' Barbara had sobbed.

Pepita had looked at her incredulously. 'You're young. You're gorgeous. You don't wear enough clothes.'

That might have been true, though at eighteen Barbara had not felt gorgeous. She had felt adolescent and clumsy, with her long, tanned legs and fall of straight, waist-length hair. She'd had no glamorous clothes, no elegant make-up. Her hands had not been soft and well cared for, and she'd frequently run about barefoot; she'd felt like the urchin the Marquês had called her.

Now, at that memory, she drew a ragged breath. Before that night she had only had one exchange with the Marquês. When she'd called on his grandmother he had either been out or working in his study. She had never met him. But one day she had been on the terrace of the Villa Branca, tidying it before she went to the stables, and Ruy had ridden past. She had looked up and seen him, a black figure against the skyline, sitting on his horse beyond the garden wall. She had the feeling he had been watching her for some time.

'Senhorinha Lamb?' His voice was clipped.

Barbara nodded.

'You come to visit my grandmother, I believe.'

She nodded again, going towards the wall behind which his horse stood so still.

'She's very kind to me.'

'I am aware.' The strange eyes lingered on her, and Barbara, who generally never thought about what she was wearing, suddenly wished desperately that she had something on that covered her more respectably than an ancient cotton shirt over a faded bikini. 'Do not try to—make use of that kindness.'

She gaped at him. She was very young, after all, and he was an impressive figure in his black riding clothes, with that savage scar and cold, imperious voice.

He said harshly into her uncomprehending face,
'She is an old lady, but she is not a fool. And nor
am I. I know your uncle, Senhorinha Lamb. If he
should approach my grandmother—in any way—I
will see him in gaol.' And, as she gasped at his
rudeness, he pushed back his wide-brimmed,
narrow hat with his riding whip in a mockery of
good manners. 'I see I make myself clear. Good
day.'

Barbara had been shaken. She had been very
hurt, though not as hurt as she was to be later. But
she'd had no way to defend herself. And the
Marquesa had stayed as gentle and welcoming as
she had always been, lending Barbara books, telling
her about the way the world was run, letting the
girl talk.

Which was why, on the awful night when Brian
Gallaher decided to collect his dues, Barbara had
run, without thinking, to the *quinta*. The Marquesa
would help. The Marquesa would shelter her. The
Marquesa would *explain* . . .

She had torn herself out of Gallaher's angry grip
and scrambled blindly off the terrace on to the wild
earth beyond the villa wall. It was dark, but it was
a clear night. In the distance she could see the lights
of the main coastal highway and, dotted over the
hills, the little lights which showed where people
lived. It was hard work going cross-country to the
quinta, especially half running and confused with
panic as she was, but it was not impossible. She
tore her skin on unseen prickles and her hair tangled
with unexpectedly low branches, but in the end she
made it.

It was the dogs who announced her arrival. They began to bark almost as soon as she was within sight of the *quinta*. She came slithering down the hillside, through the plantation of apricot and almond trees to the lemon orchard at the back of the house. She was almost exhausted then and, when she caught her foot in a fallen branch, she lay on the ground panting, unable to rise.

That was where Ruy found her. She heard the commotion, the dogs, the voices, people coming out from the building with lights that trembled in the dark, beginning to search the grounds. It was sheer bad luck that it was the Marquês who looked in the orchard. His flashlight picked her out and she heard him exclaim, 'Good God!'

Then she was looking up at him, a great wavering shadow behind the searchlight, her chest rising and falling in agony.

He put the light down carefully and picked her up. She had not realised how easily it could be done and, fresh from Gallaher's assault, she whimpered in fear. He took no notice.

In the house they cared for her. Elena saw to her hurts, clucking over her tomboyish ways, while the Marquês looked on sombrely. Eventually he waved the housekeeper away.

'You will tell me what happened, if you please,' he said the moment the door closed behind her.

Barbara flushed miserably. But she did not think of lying to him.

'It was ... I mean, Harry's gone away and ...'

'And your lover got rougher than you expected?' he said neutrally.

She bit her lip. 'I have no lover.'

'No?' He was sipping brandy, looking broodingly at her over the top of it. 'Yet you permit him familiarities.'

She knew he was talking about Brian Gallaher. She made a futile gesture with her torn hands. 'He's a business associate of Harry's. I have been friendly.'

'Like tonight?' The Marquês was contemptuous. 'Those bruises do not look very friendly to me. I don't think you got them on my almond trees.'

Barbara felt the shamed colour rise in her cheeks. 'No,' she acknowledged quietly, 'I tried, but—he wouldn't *listen*...' Her voice began to rise and she stopped, drawing several slow breaths. 'He'd been drinking, you see.'

The Marquês let out an expletive which Barbara recognised from the language of the stable boys. She stopped, startled. Surely she must have misheard? The elegant Marquês would not use such expressions, surely?

'Go on,' he told her, his voice curt.

But she could not. She was too exhausted, too lost and bewildered, and now too drained by his hammering questions.

'Please...' It was a thread of sound.

Elena came back into the room, carrying a long white robe.

'I have prepared the small tapestry room,' she said kindly. 'You will want to take off those nasty, dirty things.'

The Marquês' cool glance flicked over Barbara.
'Do you deliberately dress to look like an urchin?'
he enquired.

Oddly, it was the distaste she heard in his voice
which nearly broke her spirit. The final straw, she
supposed drearily. She was surprised to hear kindly
Elena standing up for her. The housekeeper did not
approve of her style of dress either, though she
probably suspected the penury that was responsible
for it in a way that the Marquês could not.

'The little one is still a child, Dom Ruy,' she was
saying, an odd warning note in her voice. 'Don't
be hard on her because she is sometimes a tomboy.
At her age, it is easy to forget sometimes that one
is a young lady.'

His face twisted. That was the first time Barbara
had seen the scar working as the tense muscle near
his eye pulsed. He looked as if he were in pain or
in a furious temper, either of which could result in
violence. She shrank a little against the housekeeper's shoulder.

'I don't think this time her injuries are due to
climbing trees,' he said in a voice that grated. The
cold eyes, green as the depths of his own lagoon,
rested briefly on the torn T-shirt. He added savagely, 'Nor are her age and sex hidden from plain
view. Oh, put her to bed, for God's sake!' He
stormed out of the room.

Elena looked after her like a mother. She was
gentler than Barbara remembered anyone being
with her before. She told her not to mind the
Marquês, he had a lot on his mind. He had not
meant it. He would be sorry in the morning.

And certainly in the morning he had been kinder in a remote way. The Marquesa, informed in the morning of what had happened, was shocked and disapproving. Barbara was not able to tell her everything, and she clearly thought that Gallaher's advances had shocked her because she was so young. She had no idea of Harry's sordid bargain, or the violence in the man. Barbara, shuddering, did not want to enlighten her.

The Marquesa informed her that Gallaher had been told where she was. She would, of course, stay with them until she decided what she wanted to do. She was not to worry. Ruy would see to everything. Barbara had flinched at that, but it was too late to prevent it and, anyway, the Marquês never mentioned the matter to her, though presumably he had met and talked with Gallaher.

For a week, an uneasy week in which Barbara could hardly believe her good fortune, she rested and was spoilt and slowly regained her equilibrium. And then Harry arrived, red-faced and blustering.

The first she knew of it was when she overhead loud voices in the study. Elena passed her in the passage, her face worried, hurrying towards the Marquesa's room. Everyone knew that the Marquesa must not be agitated; her heart was not strong.

'Your uncle has come,' Elena flung over her shoulder as she went.

So Barbara went to the study.

Harry was standing on the Kashmiri rug in front of the loaded desk, shouting. '... every newspaper in Europe!' he was yelling.

The Marquês' face was a mask of contempt. 'Ridiculous!'

'They'll believe me. No woman will look at you. That face scares them off, doesn't it? So you have to...' Harry saw Barbara standing in the doorway and broke off. If possible, his face turned an even deeper puce, then he strode over to her and picked up her wrist in his pudgy hand. 'Come on,' he said brusquely. 'We're leaving.'

Barbara pulled away. 'No!'

Harry stared at her. She had never defied him before. 'What do you mean?'

'I won't go with you!'

'You're crazy,' he said flatly. 'What'll you do? You've nowhere to go.'

Barbara hesitated. Suddenly his bloodshot eyes narrowed. He swung round on the Marquês, his face ugly. 'By God, you *have*...'

'Be silent!' It struck out at him like a snake.

Harry, shaken, fell silent. Barbara looked between them, alarmed.

Placatingly she said, 'Harry, I'll be all right, really I will. I'll be in touch. Only please, *please* go away now.'

Harry looked at the Marquês. 'I'll make you pay for this,' he said, incomprehensibly to Barbara. 'By God, I will!'

'I am sure you will try.' The Marquês sounded bored. He rang the embroidered bell-pull that hung behind the door. At once, almost as if he had been listening outside the door, Pedro appeared.

'Senhor Lamb is leaving. Do not admit him again,' the Marquês said in a voice like a whiplash.

He turned his back. He did not say goodbye. Embarrassed and hurt, because in his way Harry had been kind to her, Barbara kissed him awkwardly. For a moment he looked bemused, then he turned and shambled out in Pedro's wake.

She cleared her throat.

'I—er—I'm—er...'

The Marquês turned back to her. 'You're...?' he queried, eyebrows raised. He still looked ferocious, though his voice was cool as a mountain stream.

Barbara swallowed and tried again. 'I'm sorry.'

'Oh, don't be.' He gave her a savage smile and strolled towards her. 'No one has ever tried to blackmail me before. It is an interesting experience.'

'Blackmail?' She shook her head, horrified. She knew that Harry cut corners sometimes in his business dealings, but she had never thought of him as an out-and-out criminal.

The Marquês stood in front of her, looking down at her with all that old arrogance which he had dropped in the last week.

'Tell me, do you do it often? Or is this your first venture?'

Barbara stared. 'I don't understand?'

'Don't you, my little blackmailer's apprentice?' The smile was full of anger, his eyes molten.

She stepped back.

'It's quite a clever scheme, in its way. And of course, as you so cleverly guessed, I would do anything to spare my grandmother's feelings. But not blackmail.' He shook his head. 'You miscalculated there, my angel.'

The endearment was an insult. Bewildered, Barbara shook her head. 'I don't . . .'

He looked down at her. 'No, you don't, do you?' he said softly. His tone turned her blood to ice. 'That's the cream of it—to be blackmailed about something that never even happened. But it should.'

Frightened, Barbara said, 'What are you talking about?'

He reached out a hand to touch her temple in an oddly gentle gesture. 'That innocence!' He corrected himself. 'That *illusion* of innocence. You shouldn't look like that. You're a time-bomb. God knows who you'll hurt next.'

He moved very suddenly and caught her. It was like the night when he had picked her up. She felt helpless, off balance and vulnerable.

'Well, this time, my sweet, you're going to find out what happens if you blackmail people. I suspect you've been let off too often because you look . . .' He broke off. 'This time,' he finished abruptly, 'you're going to realise the consequences.'

And then he began to kiss her. It was not gentle; it was not kindly done. It made no allowance at all for her youth or emotional turmoil. At first Barbara thought he was bent on punishing her and stood still under it, hanging on to her self-control with all her strength. But then she realised there was more to it. Ruy was angry, of course, she could taste the anger in that invading mouth; furious with himself and her, exacting retribution in that comprehensive caress. But he was hungry, too. He wanted her; the questing hands were not just punishing, they were trying to wring some response out of her. And he was shaking.

In his orchard ten years later, Barbara recalled in bitter detail exactly how successful the Marquês had been in that vengeful object. She was young and ignorant, and her only previous experience of the sexual imperative had been with a man whose attack had frightened her into flight. But the Marquês was different; not because he was more skilful—though he undoubtedly was—nor because he loved her—which he undoubtedly did not. The young Barbara, when she'd recovered from her first terror, had clung to him in a frenzy of longing, recognising in this angry man her natural peer. It was crazy. Even as she'd moaned under his hands, she had known it was crazy. They were different in every possible way, age and culture and, most of all, background. Why then had she felt that he was the only man, the only possible one, ever?

She had not thought of defending herself. Though the Marquês was no less strange and frightening than Brian Gallaher, though she had never before felt what she felt now, never before known the things he was doing to her, she felt a deep sense of recognition. It might be alarming, but it was also strangely right. She responded to him with all the intensity of that sense of rightness.

In the end it was he who stopped it, he who raised his head. She remembered it as if it were last night, the strange feeling of his scar against her naked skin as he kissed her breast, the wonder of her whole body responding to his as if in a dance, and then the shock of loss when he drew back.

'Interesting,' he said coolly, though his chest was rising and falling like an athlete's and his voice was not entirely steady. 'Is this what Uncle Harry told you to do, or is it native inspiration?' And he ran his hand slowly and insultingly the length of her thigh.

Barbara had cried out, and his face had twisted. He had levered himself off her as if he could not bear to touch her, as if he had to be free of the soft arms wound pliantly round him.

He went to his desk and stood behind it, watching her. For an odd moment he looked defensive, like an animal at bay. Then he was rummaging in a drawer, not looking at her. Distressed, Barbara sat up, trying to pull her clothing back into order.

'You must go,' Ruy said rapidly. 'That's what you want, I know. Back to England.' He had some notes in his hand. He held them out across the desk with an impatient gesture.

Barbara looked blindly at the money. They were sterling notes. He thrust them at her. A black-mailer, he had called her: so he was paying her off. She felt sick.

'Take it,' he said, in a voice that burned like acid. 'Take it and go.'

She did so, of course. What else was there to do? She went at once, hardly knowing where, though she ended up at the stables, where Pepita took one look at her and gathered her in like an injured animal.

She had not told Pepita why she was fleeing. Pepita would never have believed it. Barbara did not quite believe it herself: not the revelation of Harry's petty villainy, not the burning hunger she had discovered in herself, not the pain of that vicious rejection.

In all the years afterwards, most of that week had come into perspective, but not that final, cruel exchange. Whenever a man came close, Barbara remembered how she had been in the arms of Ruy Nieves dos Santos, and she froze. In the end, she took care that no man came close.

Perhaps she had been wrong to do that. Perhaps that was why the pain was still there, buried but fatal. Perhaps that was why even now she could not bear to remember.

In the rising sunlight, Barbara turned her head against the back of the tree. Her cheek was wet. If the pain was still there, so was the fascination, heaven help her; the fascination and the hunger.

Across the orchard she heard steps, and for a moment she shrank into her hiding place. She knew who it was. Ruy could not have slept either. She watched painfully as he came into view.

He was scanning the orchard. He was dressed untidily in riding breeches and a casual shirt that he was still buttoning, as if he had pulled on the first things that had come to hand. His scar was pronounced and he looked very tired.

She stepped out from under the branches, and as soon as he saw her his eyes lightened. Then, immediately, all expression was banished. He held out his hand to her.

'You don't need to run away,' Ruy told her. 'I—misunderstood. Don't be alarmed. It won't happen again.'

CHAPTER EIGHT

THINGS did not really change after that, Barbara decided, but she became more careful. Ruy should have no more cause for misunderstanding.

Ruy himself did not seem to notice. He still kept her by his side during the day, still spent every evening teaching her about family history, playing backgammon with her and teasing her about her English accent. If he looked tired, it must be because he was working hard, retiring to his study when she went to bed and back at his desk before she got up in the morning.

She remonstrated.

'I have a lot to catch up on,' he said equably. 'I spent too much time running around after Luis this summer, and Felicia. I have a whole series of results to go through, and a paper to write.'

'Results?' echoed Barbara, bewildered. 'Do you do the football pools?'

He gave her that wonderful grin. 'No, though the pools would probably be no more difficult. I'm a physicist.' At her stare, his smile widened. 'Really! I work part-time at the university in Lisbon, part-time in Geneva. And here when I need to think.'

'Here?' She was astounded. 'But don't you need a laboratory or something?'

Ruy gave a shout of laughter. 'I do, indeed. And a nuclear reactor and a centrifugal force plant and... well, one or two things that come a little expensive. Hence Geneva. They,' he explained mock-innocently, 'do the cooking and I write the books.'

Barbara laughed, but she was thoughtful. It was a new side of his character for which she was unprepared. She had thought that, apart from his duties on the estate, which were hardly arduous, he was some sort of businessman. 'Or an international playboy,' she added.

They were out riding in the cool of the morning. His eyebrows flew up. 'Whatever gave you that idea?'

'Oh...' She looked away. Himself, of course, that devastating charm, the easy sophistication. 'The tales they told.'

'Gossip?' He sounded amused. 'I'm afraid I'm not much of a subject. The people round here used to have a much better time with my father. Now he was a real Casino Charlie.'

Barbara choked. 'A *what*?'

'Casino Charlie,' Ruy repeated. 'Monte Carlo was his second home. A lady on every polo field,' he added thoughtfully, 'or so they say.'

'Good heavens!' She stole a curious look at him. He looked very handsome, broad-shouldered in the snowy shirt that flapped a little in the early morning breeze wafting in from the sea. 'Do you take after him?'

'Well, I'm no gambler, if that's what you mean. As for the ladies—it's hardly likely, is it, looking like one of Frankenstein's rejects?'

Barbara's horse started forward; she must have jerked on the reins. She could not help it: her heart contracted in fury and pity when he sounded like that. She said carefully, 'How did it happen? I've never known.'

Ruy looked down at her absently. He seemed very far away all at once.

'My scar? Oh——' For a moment she thought he wouldn't answer, then he shrugged. 'It was on a fishing trip—a knife slipped. I was lucky.'

'Lucky?'

He gave her an unsmiling glance. 'Not to lose the eye. At least I can see, even if I'm not too decorative to be seen.'

'When—when did it happen?' she faltered, feeling sick.

'Don't look like that,' he said under his breath.

'What?' Barbara was bewildered.

But he was shaking himself, answering her question.

'Not so long before you came here—twelve, thirteen years ago. Now, if you'd accused me of being a playboy then, it might have been true. I was sowing a few wild oats in those days.'

And it all came to an end with his injury. He did not have to say it. Barbara wanted to touch him, and found she did not quite have the courage.

'Where did it happen?' she asked.

'Where? Oh, you mean geographically. Here. We were out in a boat.' He nodded towards the sea, which was creaming away to their left. 'We were having a house party. It—rather spoilt the fun.'

He would have been devastating then, she thought: mid-twenties, young and strong and full of energy, with that wildly handsome face and lithe body.

'It made me grow up rather suddenly,' Ruy said. 'Probably not before time.'

She said, 'I'm so sorry,' trying to pretend that her voice was not thick with tears and making rather a bad job of it.

He said fiercely, 'Don't feel sorry for me. It taught me more about people in one blow than the whole of the rest of my life put together.'

Barbara thought it had not taught him to like or trust them very much. She said slowly, 'Is that why you're only really happy here? Because you are, aren't you?'

He stiffened for a moment. Then, quite suddenly, he relaxed, saying simply, 'Yes.'

'You were different in London. I thought . . . But I was wrong. It's here. You're on your home territory.'

He slanted a look down at her. 'Like the proverbial wounded animal, I suppose.' His voice was full of self-mockery. 'But you're right, though you're the first person to have noticed it.'

She realised sadly how much he must have wanted to marry Pepita, then. Pepita was part of his place where he was at home and safe. Pepita was not part

of the callous outside world where he was stared at
and reviled. Barbara recalled Trevor's callous insult,
and her hands clenched on the reins again. But for
her Ruy would not have had to endure that.

She said sadly, half to herself, 'I wish I were the
right wife for you.'

Ruy did not answer. They clopped along for a
moment, their horses' hoofs striking the earth with
a dull sound, sending up a dust spray on the arid
hilltop path. He was looking out over the sea.

At last he said slowly, 'I don't think I believe in
things like "the right wife", the right decision. Life
isn't like one of Luis' schoolbooks, with the answers
in the back. There are no answers. We just do the
best we can with what we have.'

It sounded bleak to Barbara. She persisted, 'But
you must have an idea of what you really want,
mustn't you? What you would take if you could
have anything in the world?'

He shot her a quick look. 'And what you would
pay for it?'

She made an impatient gesture. 'Yes, all right.
What you would pay for it. Everything has to be
paid for, one way or another.' She guided the horse
carefully down a particularly steep stretch of track.
The she said, 'What would you really want, Ruy?
If you could choose?'

He was so long in answering that she thought he
would ignore her. But at last he said, in a tone that
seemed to have been hacked out of him, 'I had it
once—or nearly. And I wasn't entitled to it, even
then.'

Barbara stared. 'What do you mean?'

Ruy said with difficulty, 'If what you want depends on—someone else—you can't just take. If they don't want it, then——' he shrugged, 'you have to accept it.'

Against her will, Barbara's eyes went to the long low building that was the house and stables where Pepita lived. She pressed her lips tightly together. It was becoming more and more obvious that Pepita had hurt him badly. And she, Barbara, had had a hand in that too. She hung her head.

'I'm sorry,' she said again, guilt in every line of her.

The man's mouth twisted. The tall, beautiful body in the saddle seemed to brace itself, though Barbara did not see it, but when he spoke his voice was a miracle of calm.

'Don't worry. There are some things we can't help.'

She noticed that the rest of the day he avoided her. And kept his scar turned away.

They got back to the *quinta* to find a letter waiting from Luis. It was more dutiful than expressive, and only really came to life when he described his sub-aqua lessons. Ruy snorted, throwing the letter across the tea-tray for Barbara to read.

'That boy is laziness personified!'

Barbara scanned the ill-spelt letter. 'Should we have him home, then?'

Ruy considered. 'Eventually, yes. We'll have to employ some sort of schoolmaster to bring him up to scratch, I suppose. He can't go to school here.'

She was faintly shocked. 'Why not?'

He gave her an ironic look. 'You haven't met the little monster. He'd bully all his schoolmates. He has a thoroughly unhealthy habit of talking about *"my uncle, the Marquês"*. He needs to go to some school where they'll sit on him when he does. England, I think. I looked into it while I was there.'

'Will he feel I've ousted him from his rightful home?' asked Barbara uneasily.

'He's ousted himself,' said Ruy callously, 'by doing no work and worrying Felicia into a collapse.'

Barbara said tentatively, 'Do you dislike him?'

Ruy frowned. 'I don't know much about children. And his father——' He broke off. 'No, you can't blame a child,' he said, almost as if he were trying to convince himself.

Barbara felt her heart sink. But she said brightly, 'What does he want to be when he grows up? A *marquês*?'

Ruy shook his head, relaxing a little. 'No, thank God. That really would worry me. At the moment he can't make up his mind whether he wants to be a world surfer champion or the greatest inventor in the universe. Both,' he added with a return to gloom, 'would be too much work for him, I suspect.'

Barbara laughed and said she refused to be daunted. Which was just as well, because Ruy clearly looked forward to his nephew's return with a trepidation which was only partly a joke.

She realised why as soon as they met the boy at the airport. He was a cheerful, confident teenager, very blond and open, and he could not bear to look at Ruy. Barbara remembered Ruy telling her as much, but she was astounded at how shocking it was to see in the flesh. The only thing that made it bearable was the fact that the boy was evidently acutely unhappy about it, and had no idea of the effect his aversion had on his uncle.

In pity, she watched time and again as Ruy made some approach to the boy, only to meet that blank response. And then, of course, Ruy would lose his temper and Luis would start to squirm and they were back at square one. Barbara tried to mediate, without any great success.

But on her own she got on easily enough with Luis. It was he who challenged her frankly on Ruy's fine-drawn appearance. Although he could not look his uncle in the face, he was not unobservant, obviously.

'Uncle Ruy's pretty chewed up, isn't he?' he said casually, after one of their games of tennis. 'Is being married getting him down?'

Barbara had been watching Ruy herself in anxiety, seeing the skin stretched over his elegant bones as if he had somehow used up all the flesh and now was living on pure will alone. She was very afraid that it was his reaction to the loss of Pepita. She did not dare to bring the subject up, but she found she knew in her bones a lot about Ruy. For instance, she knew how he would deal with unwelcome emotion. He would drive himself to death and laugh. Which was exactly what he was

doing. It hurt her to see. And here was this child
seeing it too.

She said as lightly as she could manage, 'Do you
think he's one of nature's bachelors, then?'

The boy looked at her solemnly, and she realised
that he was not as young as he sometimes liked to
appear. The clear young face was worried.

'I guess not. Though—my parents used to say he
couldn't find a wife.'

It was an odd thing for a child to be allowed to
overhear; even odder that he remembered it.
Barbara looked at him curiously. It was obviously
a memory he disliked.

'Because he's so ugly,' he went on, trying to
sound casual and succeeding only in a sort of scared
misery. He swallowed. 'My father gave him that
scar, you know.'

Barbara was horrified. She whispered, 'Oh no!'
her hand flying to her own cheek.

Luis looked at her defiantly. 'Makes him look
like Frankenstein's monster or something, doesn't
it?' he said with bravado. He did a monster's walk
along the edge of the tennis court.

Barbara could not have laughed to save her life.
He stopped and came back to her.

'*How?*' she said, more to herself than anyone
else. It was hardly likely that Luis would know, but
he did.

'They had a fight. Uncle Ruy lifted my dad's
girlfriend,' he said with shocking nonchalance. 'My
dad——' it was clearly straight recall from his

father's account '——said he'd spoil his pretty face. And he did.'

The echo of the dead man's boastfulness was chilling. Barbara knew she whitened. Luis gave her a shamed look, his eyes sliding sideways away from her. It was what he did to Ruy. Why, thought Barbara, enlightened, he's not horrified by the scar, he's *ashamed*!

Instinctively she put her arms round him. Up to now she had been scrupulous not to embarrass him with physical demonstration, out of respect to their new relationship and his mature years. Now she did not even think of it. Luis returned her hug enthusiastically.

'Dad said that's how men settle their debts,' he said in a small voice.

Barbara was suddenly very angry. 'It may be how nasty schoolboys settle their debts,' she said, 'not men.' She smoothed his hair. 'Ask Uncle Ruy if you don't believe me.'

Luis raised his head. His eyes were wet.

'I couldn't talk to him about it,' he said with absolute conviction. He looked appalled at the very thought. 'He must *hate* me.'

'Hate you? Why?'

Luis swallowed. 'My dad. And him—looking like that. It's true about girls too. Pepita couldn't stand it.' Something occurred to him, and he looked at her, puzzled, momentarily distracted. 'Don't you mind?'

'No,' Barbara said steadily after a minute. 'No, I don't mind.'

'My mom did.' Luis was back with his memories. 'She wouldn't have him in their wedding pictures, you know. Or at my christening. Great-Gran told me that.'

Barbara said, 'Luis, do *you* mind?'

He looked startled.

'I mean, does it make your stomach turn over every time you look at your uncle?'

'No,' he said, clearly bewildered.

'Then that's all that matters. Not your parents. You, and how you feel.'

He was unconvinced, she could see. She felt helpless. She did not know what else to say. If she told him not to flinch away every time his uncle spoke to him, she would only make him more self-conscious.

In the end, she decided to speak to Ruy. She chose her moment carefully. They had been riding together at a whirlwind gallop along the beach, his hair flying as he crouched low over his horse's neck. Now, breathing hard, he was looking relaxed and less tense than she had seen him for days.

'Ruy.'

'Yes?'

Barbara edged her horse close to his, which was cropping blissfully at a crop of sea grasses. She plunged in.

'Did you know that Luis knows how you were injured?'

He turned blank green eyes on her. For a moment he looked horrified.

'His father told him,' Barbara said quietly, presenting him with the evidence.

Ruy closed his eyes.

'Luis thinks you must blame him—hate him.'

The eyes flew open. 'What do you mean?' Ruy asked in a dry whisper.

She felt a flicker of temper. 'I mean the poor child's eaten up with guilt each time he sees you.'

Not so very unlike herself, she thought, remembering the part she had played in helping Pepita break the engagement; and then parting him utterly from his true love for ever.

'Guilt? But why on earth...?'

'He can see you're unhappy,' she said in an even voice. She could have been talking about herself. 'And he feels he's a contributory factor. He's ashamed, and he doesn't know how to put things right. So he tries to keep out of your way.'

Ruy's expression was black. 'Damn Fernando,' he said between his teeth. 'He was always irresponsible; but why the hell he had to tell the child...'

Remembering her own feeling that Fernando had been proud of his exploit, Barbara held her tongue.

'It seems,' said Ruy grimly, 'that Luis and I are due for a talk.'

'Don't frighten him,' said Barbara involuntarily.

He gave her a disgusted look and refused to say more, shaking his reluctant horse into activity and hurrying back to the *quinta*.

But the next time she saw them it was clear her fears had been unfounded. They were walking together by the edge of the creek where Ruy kept the boats, talking hard.

As she approached, Barbara heard Luis say, '... and I was just getting quite good.'

'In whose estimation, yours or your teacher's?' asked Ruy. He sounded cool but not unfriendly. Luis did not appear to be intimidated.

'The teacher. Still, she could have wanted me to keep going for lessons, I guess,' he added fairly.

Ruy laughed. 'Very shrewd. All right! If you can prove to me that you are sufficiently proficient not to drown yourself, I will finance more lessons. *If* you also turn out some schoolwork.'

Luis grinned up at him, his eyes brilliant. Barbara caught her breath. For the first time he was looking Ruy in the face.

'That's bribery. You're not supposed to bribe kids to work.'

Ruy himself looked arrested. 'Who says?' he said at last.

'My child psychologist,' said Luis with a professional air. He gave another of his grins. It made him look startlingly like his uncle.

'I think,' Ruy said drily, 'I'm going to introduce you to Machiavelli.'

'Who's he? A scuba diver?' asked Luis, all eagerness.

'A sixteenth-century Italian writer with whom you have one or two things in common,' his uncle informed him. He ruffled the boy's hair, in an odd shy gesture that showed he had not done it before.

Barbara caught her breath. But Luis accepted it sunnily.

'Oh, schoolwork.'

'Wait till you read him,' said Ruy. 'Even you may have something to learn from him. Come to my study after lunch and we'll start.'

'We?'

Ruy grinned down at him. 'If I don't refresh my memory, you're going to get ahead. And then I won't be master in my own home any more. Can't risk it. We'll read it together.'

His nephew looked equally surprised and pleased, but all he said was, 'OK,' in an offhand tone.

Barbara, reading the tone as clearly as Ruy did, went up to them, making no comment on the change in relations.

It was a great pleasure to see Ruy happy in Luis' company, as she did increasingly in the following weeks. It compensated to some extent for his increasing tension. She thought he was working too hard, but when she ventured to say so he retorted so fiercely that they almost had an argument. But when the Marquesa arrived from her London clinic she said the same thing.

Ruy glared at them both impartially.

'I am not tired. I am not ill. I am not working too hard. In fact, I was thinking it was time we celebrated this marriage of ours,' he said to Barbara. 'A dance, I think, here at the *quinta*. Neighbours and one or two English friends. Fancy dress—I like to cut a swagger behind a mask. It's the next best thing to being left alone by your family.'

And he stamped off to the library.

The Marquesa sighed, and pulled a face at Barbara.

Barbara was not amused. She had heard in that irritated voice an echo of something deeper and more desolate than irritation. Ruy was lacking his true love, and her heart ached for him. She knew what it was like, and it was so unfair that they should nag him to appear cheerful when his heart was broken.

She stopped herself dead in the middle of the thought. She knew what it was like? What was this? She had never been in love in her life! That dreadful encounter here in this house, with this very man, had effectively prevented it. She had kept her love safely packed in ice for ten years. Nobody had got close enough to touch her heart.

But, if nobody had got close enough, why was she sitting here fighting tears because she knew Ruy hurt?

The answer was horribly, frighteningly obvious. He might be in love with Pepita, but it made no difference. Barbara loved him; had probably loved him for ten years without knowing it.

That was why she had felt that sense of inevitability when they had met again. That was why she was willing to give up her life and marry him. It had nothing to do with convenience. She had been in love with him all along. She recalled how she always wanted to hold him when he spoke so bit-

terly of his disfigurement. Now she saw it for what
it was: Love, and the need to succour the beloved.
She must have been mad not to realise it before.

So she could not return the Marquesa's conspira-
torial smile. Under the old lady's thoughtful gaze
she gave a blind, meaningless smile and made a
rapid exit.

She walked in the cooling garden, her cheeks
aflame. Had Ruy guessed? Did it disgust him? Or
was it irrelevant in his despair over Pepita? Now
she understood clearly why she could not bear him
to make love to her. It was nothing to do with her
own fastidiousness, her fear of physical and
emotional involvement. It was because, every time
he touched her, she wanted a whole dragon's
treasury more than he could offer her.

Oh, heavens, she thought, what a mess! Poor
Ruy. And what a fool not to perceive her own
feelings. How could she have been so blind, so
criminally stupid? There was only one thing she
could do—make sure that he never felt her love as
a burden. He had married for support, to share
responsibility, he wouldn't want to shoulder the
unwanted affection of an idiot who hadn't the wit
to know herself.

Her new resolve was not easy to carry out, but
she did her best. Although it hurt to forgo a single
minute in Ruy's company, she began to avoid him.
The strain of guarding her tongue and, worse, her
expression, was too great.

She wondered whether he had noticed. Sometimes she was certain of it, when his eyes rested on

her ironically as she found some excuse not to ride with him. At others, when he accepted without question her plea of preoccupation with the arrangements for the dance he had insisted on, she thought not. The dance certainly encroached more and more on her time. There was a huge chart in the kitchen of things to be collected, people to be met, rooms to be used and food to be set out. In the bustle she almost forgot to provide herself with a costume. Ruy had had his way, and it was to be a fancy-dress party.

'It's easy,' said the Marquesa comfortably when close questioning revealed that Barbara had forgotten the necessity and was about to panic. 'There are plenty of things in the cupboards. I saved everything, and so did my mother-in-law. I always hoped for a daughter who would have enjoyed dressing up. Now,' with a warm smile, 'I have one.'

So they went up to the empty rooms in the east wing and spent an entertaining hour rifling through sheeted gowns in its ancient wardrobes. It was fairly clear to Barbara that the Marquesa was looking for one particular dress. Eventually she found it, and Barbara gasped.

It was at first sight a flapper's dress, skimpily cut, leaving much of the shoulders and bosom bare, with a handkerchief skirt that at its highest was cut to the thigh.

'It's indecent!' gasped Barbara, as her companion removed its cotton covering.

'Yes,' agreed the Marquesa with pleasure. 'And so pretty.'

She swirled it out and Barbara saw that it was printed, presumably by hand, with a pattern of a cobweb in silky grey filaments. As the skirt flared, the dress turned into an exquisitely lacy web.

'It's magic!' said Barbara, awed. She touched the material with a reverent finger. 'It must be worth a fortune.'

The Marquesa nodded complacently. 'Sergio bought it for me in Paris. It was his favourite. It will give me great happiness if you wear it.'

So Barbara agreed. If she were honest, she had other things on her mind than her costume for the dance. The post that had brought acceptances of their invitations had also brought a message from Harry. He was glad that his niece had had the good sense to marry a rich man. He was in a bit of trouble himself at the moment. He would be looking her up soon, though.

She wondered whether to show it to Ruy. He had promised to protect her from her uncle's attentions, and she believed him. But he was busy, and she was wary of approaching too close lest she betray herself. So she said nothing and the letter yellowed in her drawer.

And then, the morning before the dance, when Ruy was out riding and she was taking her lonely morning stroll along the clifftop, Harry appeared.

Barbara stopped dead. It made her heart sink, just the sight of his cheerful, shifty face.

'Hello, my dear,' he greeted her. 'Thought you'd pass this way—I've been watching you.' And he indicated the binoculars round his neck.

Barbara flushed, but said steadily, 'Spying, Harry? What do you want?'

He managed to look hurt. 'Would I spy on my little girl? I just want to be sure you're happy, with that scarfaced bastard.'

Barbara murmured, 'Careful, Harry! I thought he was St Moneybags of Rock.'

Harry managed to look shocked this time, shocked and virtuous. 'I don't like to hear you talk like that. You were never mercenary as a child. Not like your poor father.' Her smile faded. 'Couldn't get enough of it, no matter who paid—even his own flesh and blood.'

Barbara turned away in disgust. 'God, what a family I come from!'

He sidled round to face her again. 'Well, I thought that myself when I heard you'd married him. He can't know, I said to myself. My little Barbara can't have told him. Easy enough to understand. I wouldn't tell him myself if...'

The sentence trailed off, its message depressingly clear. Barbara looked at him wearily. 'Blackmail, Harry?'

He did not try to deny it, though he said with what he thought was a winning smile, 'Bit of help for your old uncle?'

She thought of Ruy, his pride and his upright dealings. How he would hate this. She would not humble him by contact with this creature, she *would* not. She turned away.

'Barbara...' He sounded astonished, padding after her after a moment.

'Do what you want, Harry,' she flung at him,
striding over the turf. 'I told you last time that it
was the last. You should have believed me.'

'But . . .'

She swung round and said fiercely, 'I won't have
you leeching off my husband the way you have off
me all these years. Go away!'

'But he can afford it,' said Harry in honest and
rather laughable bewilderment.

'Maybe,' Barbara said cryptically, 'but I can't.
You come anywhere near us again and rather than
make him pay you, I swear I'll leave him if I have
to!'

'You're mad,' said Harry, falling back.

And she was, she thought, pelting down the
hillside; mad with love. And it was getting no better.

There were now almost no subjects on which she
dared to speak to Ruy. Pepita was coming to the
dance, a subject on which he had expressed no views
whatsoever. She could not tell whether he was in
despair, or whether just the sight of the Spanish
girl was worth the pain. She tried to ask, but failed
miserably.

'Worth it?' he said to her careful hypothetical
question. 'Who knows? It depends on your
temperament, I suppose. You must have been in
love. Do you regret it?'

She thought of those brief moments in his arms,
the bitterness of his rejection, ten lonely years and
the tortured tightrope of the present. Would she
rather never have felt that surge of feeling?

'No,' she said with absolute assurance. 'No, it was worth whatever it cost.'

He put his hand over his eyes. 'I'd probably say the same,' he said gratingly. 'Sometimes.'

She did not dare to ask any more. She was not sure she could bear the answers. Instead she asked him about his appearance at the party.

'Oh, I've already got my costume. I've had it for ages. That's why I wanted a fancy-dress party.'

'What is it?'

Ruy looked mischievous. 'Guess.'

'A pierrot?'

He shook his head. 'I'm not a conventional Englishman.'

She wrinkled her nose at him. 'A cavalier. Louis the Fourteenth. Fu Manchu.'

He shook his head again.

'I give up. Tell me.'

'No, wait and see. You'll be dazzled.'

Barbara laughed and promised to be suitably dazzled. She was intrigued. Ruy was not normally a peacock, and this secrecy about what he was going to wear struck her as uncharacteristic.

When he came downstairs on the night of the party, she understood the reason for it, however. She began to laugh.

At first, as her husband descended the staircase, she had thought he was not in costume at all. He was wearing slim-fitting grey trousers, which moulded his legs, and a long-sleeved grey jacket buttoned to the neck from a point just above the waistband.

'A ghost?' Barbara said quizzically.

Then, from behind his back, Ruy produced the mask. It was a cat's face, a great whiskered grey face with its three-cornered mouth in a bland smile and its eyes hunting wide and yellow. He slipped it on and put up a hand to flourish at a proud whisker.

Barbara laughed until she had a stitch in her side. 'Have you got a tail?'

He slid the mask off, chuckling. 'Yes. Luis is going to attach it for me.'

Luis, in on the joke and hugely enjoying himself, arrived. He was wearing a marmalade-striped jumpsuit and fur paws. Barbara saw that any hope she had of persuading him to go to bed at something approaching a normal time had disappeared. Uncle and nephew were going hunting as a pair.

'I hope to God none of our guests comes as a mouse,' Barbara said, putting on her own mask of velvet and stiffened lace. It stood out from her face like a Venetian half-mask, and was so light she almost forgot she was wearing it after half an hour.

'You look very beautiful,' Ruy told her carelessly. He slanted a look down at her before he put his own mask back on. 'I wonder if cats chase spiders?'

Barbara's heart began to beat shatteringly hard, and she quelled it.

'I'm not a spider,' she said firmly, 'I'm a cobweb. Altogether more romantic.'

He gave her a little mock bow. 'I apologise, Senhora Marquesa.'

And then he and Luis whirled away and the guests began to arrive.

Dick and Alanna were staying in the house, of course. Alanna was Cinderella before the transformation because, as she pointed out practically, on a hot Portuguese night it was a nice cool costume. Dick was a pirate. There were plenty of other pirates; it was a relatively easy costume to fabricate. He went round challenging other pirates to duels. Luis, in seventh heaven, dashed between him and his uncle.

Ruy was having great fun stalking under tables and jumping out from beneath the tablecloth at his unsuspecting guests. Luis went one better and chased the shoelace of a Spanish grandee, managing to bring down both the grandee, the grandee's partner and an adjacent table with his success. Fortunately everyone was enjoying themselves too much to complain, after the first surprise.

Pepita arrived with a group of others from the area. She was Helen of Troy, another cool costume, with her hair elaborately pinned on top of her head, leaving just a few curls at the back of her neck. She looked infinitely happier than when Barbara had last seen her, and it caused her a stab of pain. The same could hardly be said for Ruy.

Pepita kissed Barbara. 'Lovely,' she said, looking round the courtyard, hung with its coloured lights. On the veranda above, the musicians were playing a lively samba. 'Beautifully done. And what a gorgeous dress! Ruy's extravagance?'

Barbara smiled. 'Ruy paid me the statutory compliment, but he's having too much fun on the tiles himself this evening to bother about anything else. He thought I was a spider.'

Pepita laughed. In the distance Ruy was butting his head against the hip of a substantial Empress Josephine. 'Oh, he's in one of those moods, is he? God help us all! Still, I suppose you'll be able to stop him if he wants to walk a tightrope across the courtyard or something.'

Barbara was startled. 'Is that a possibility?'

'He's done it before,' Pepita said blithely. 'When he gets the devil in him, he goes utterly out of control. Still,' she added happily to Barbara's profound consternation, 'you'll be able to stop him now he's a sober married man.'

Barbara looked at the sober married man, winding himself round the Empress Josephine in order to urge her on to the dance-floor.

'Yes,' she said in a hollow voice.

Fortunately she was too busy greeting guests, looking after the older ladies and seeing that the Marquesa did not overtire herself, to worry whether Ruy was going to become acrobatic. For the next hour she was the conscientious hostess. For an hour after that she danced, drank a little, circulated and danced again. The music was strongly rhythmic, with a pagan, insistent beat that compelled her on to the floor again and again.

'You're terrific,' a puffing pirate told her between gyrations. 'I see why Ruy married you.'

'Thank you,' Barbara said sweetly.

'He's the best dancer on the floor. Always has been, since we were boys,' the rotund Englishman confided.

'He's the only one on all fours,' she pointed out, allowing him to lead her off the floor.

But Ruy was upright now and dancing with all the skill that his lithe body could command. He looked magnificent, of course. Every time she looked at him Barbara felt that catch of the throat. She was coming to fear it almost more than anything she had ever known. If Ruy ever realised . . .

The unconventional costume suited him. Among all the pirates and musketeers, he looked supple and dangerous, the slim grey trousers making his legs look longer and more lithe than any human's. As he danced he had the wild, violent grace of the animal he had chosen. And the mask—the scornful, haughty mask—was a masterpiece.

Barbara smoothed her own pale skirts with fingers that shook a little. She was looking good, she knew; probably better than she ever had in her life. Although Ruy had not really noticed, many of her guests had already complimented her. And on the face of at least one of her partners she had seen a look that was a far more potent tribute than any words.

None of it made any difference. She was still that sad eighteen-year-old, caught in the grip of cruel claws, fighting she knew not what, defeated before she had even realised she had to fight. Watching Ruy, his hands on the bare back of a tanned Cleopatra, Barbara felt her mouth go dry. She had thought it was fear ten years ago. Well, she knew better now.

Suddenly the air was stifling. The night was still, warm and scented, saturated with the jasmine that clung to the ancient walls. The coloured lanterns cast an unearthly light on the dancers, adding their own heat to the atmosphere. In the heat, many of the dancers had discarded their masks. Barbara put up exploratory fingers to her own, reluctant to abandon her disguise. No, the scrap of stiffened velvet and lace was still there.

Ruy had not taken off his own mask either. Even while he danced he kept the broad, unchanging smile between himself and the world. Not that he was expressionless tonight, Barbara thought, on a twist of pain. His face might be hidden, but his body had never been more eloquent. She watched as he circled the gyrating Cleopatra, intent, predatory, intensely tactile. His hands snaked out, just touched the girl's golden skin, spun her in a ferocious arc, steadied her and fell. Barbara swallowed.

The cat mask turned towards her, and instinctively she stepped back, further into the shadows at the edge of the dance floor. Her skirt swirled, flecked with purple, green and flame under the party lights.

Across the dancers, the sinuous cat figure went very still.

Slowly, reluctantly, Barbara raised her eyes. She could not see Ruy properly. There were a hundred people dancing and talking between them, but their eyes locked. She felt her skin flinch, as if he had touched a poniard to it.

Oh God, she thought frantically. He would know now. He *had* to know. There was no way she could hide it, standing there dazed, while her thoughts scurried and her feet refused to move.

Ruy turned away from Cleopatra as if she did not exist. Not taking his eyes from Barbara's, he made his way through the throng as if he did not notice them. He moved like a cat too, she thought, with long, graceful strides, perfectly poised, exquisitely lithe. Despite the crowd and the clumsy dancing, he did not so much as touch his shoulder against any of the revellers as he passed them. When he stood in front of her, none of his guests had even noticed that he'd passed.

For a long moment there was silence between them. It was a silence that was almost tangible, a quite different state of being from the pulsating music and laughter only a few feet away. Barbara felt unreal. She was suspended in a glass bubble. She had forgotten how to move, how to think. She had forgotten everything except how to stare endlessly into shadowed eyes she could not even see.

Ruy put up a hand and wrenched off his mask.

CHAPTER NINE

BARBARA drew in a breath. Ruy bent his head as if she had spoken and he had to stoop to catch the words. Behind his dark figure the party eddied and flowed. She saw beyond his shoulder that their guests were still dancing, oblivious of the still corner in which the hosts stood locked in silence. It seemed they had become invisible.

Ruy said softly, almost pleadingly, 'Come with me.'

Faintly surprised at her own action, Barbara gave him her hand. He took it between both of his own, casting the cat mask away from him impatiently, searching her face.

Then suddenly he turned and was pulling her after him, out of the crowd, away from the music and the food and the lights, and into the scented darkness of the garden. Behind them the house on its slope looked like a toy, with its brilliantly lit windows and perfect arrangement of columns and wings.

It soon faded into silence. Ruy went determinedly towards the shore. Barbara stumbled a little on the path, which was uneven and baked dry by the summer sun. He did not slacken his pace.

At last he reached his goal, the small gate which led from the garden on to their private beach and the banks of the creek where Luis went fishing. There he stopped and turned, propping himself against its ancient hinges, holding her away from him.

'Tell me...'

It was hardly more than a breath, softer than the lulling of the sea out of sight before them, softer than the faint breeze in the orchard behind them.

'Yes?' Barbara was whispering too.

'Do you—want this?' he said with difficulty.

She did not pretend to misunderstand. She stepped forward so that her body under the Marquesa's silk was touching his. Involuntarily, his arms went round her. His hands slid under the raggedy sleeves so that his fingers lay against her flesh. She shivered voluptuously, and Ruy pulled her against him.

His cheek touched her hair, as he said her name. He sounded shaken.

It was hopeless. There was too much love, too much feeling too long suppressed. If she only had this night—if it embarrassed them both fatally and for ever—it did not make any difference: she could no more resist than she could have turned into a fish and swum away.

Knowing she would have to pay for it, Barbara put her hands very tenderly to cup his face. Under her sensitive fingertips, she felt his scar's roughness and the tension in him. She stood up on tiptoe and brushed her lips across the scar's cruel length.

This time he did not push her away.

For hectic moments Barbara lost all sense of who or where she was. When he lifted his head, she was vaguely surprised to find herself upright and on dry land. She told him so, and he gave a husky laugh.

'Not for long,' he said in a voice so loving that she hardly recognised it.

She gave a little anticipatory shiver, half delight, half despair. There was no going back now, she knew it. To still her own fears, to reach for some sort of normality, she said teasingly, 'Ruy Nieves, I am not making love for the first time on a lilo!'

He laughed again, the sound deep and resonant, but not without a tremor in it. Ruy was no more in command of himself than she was.

'Indeed you are not.'

He felt behind him to unlatch the gate, and swung it open. Not taking his eyes from her shadowed face, he drew her through and on to the mossy riverbank. Beyond, she knew, among the willows, was a small boat which Luis was forbidden to approach. She wondered sharply if it was where Ruy took all his ladies.

'What is it?' he asked swiftly.

Barbara shook her head, shocked to find that her disconcerting thought had transmitted itself to him.

'I stumbled,' she said, though they both knew it was not true.

And it did not matter. She knew about the other ladies, anyway. Even if it had not been for the gossip, she would have guessed. How else would he have perfected that devastating skill, so that his merest touch turned her into a wild thing?

The bankside vegetation all but hid the craft. Barbara hesitated, looking at the steeply angled plank set against its side with nervousness. Without a second's hesitation Ruy swung her off her feet and held her high against his chest, laughing. Well, she supposed they did not need any particular telepathy for him to have guessed her feelings there.

The interior of the boat was total blackness. For some reason Ruy did not light a light, though he must have known where it was. Instead they stumbled hand in hand into the cabin, laughing under their breath like children on an illicit outing.

All the time Barbara was conscious of the warmth of his body, the strength in the sinewy hand, the iron protectiveness of his arm when he threw it about her shoulders. For all the groping and bumping into things, he made sure she did not hurt herself. She followed him trustfully.

The cabin was small, and they had to stand close as they rid themselves of their clothes. Barbara shivered at the cool air on her heated skin, then turned thankfully into the concealing warmth of Ruy's embrace. They tumbled on to the unseen bunk, mouths locked, arms tight about each other.

It was not, she thought muzzily, what she had ever expected in her wildest dreams. The gentle rocking of the boat, the tarry smell, the harshness of some rough blanket beneath her, were all sensations no less improbable than the urgent body of the man she loved. She had never imagined either that it would be in her power to stir him into groaning need. For all his remote incalculability, he was trembling in her arms like a boy, seeking her mouth almost clumsily with bruising hunger.

The last vestiges of dismay dissolved. She responded without reserve, filled with awe as she heard him gasp at her touch. Their bodies could not keep apart, they plunged together with a searing force that swamped pain and fear alike. Barbara shut her eyes and clung to him, hearing herself cry out, hearing Ruy.

They fell asleep, inextricably entwined. Once, some time later, she thought she felt him stir. She had the impression he was settling her against him, pulling up some coverlet against the cold. More than half asleep, she burrowed against him, murmuring her pleasure. She sank back into dreams, feeling more cared for than she had ever before in her life.

In the morning Barbara woke slowly in a daze. First of all she felt cramped. Then, as she stretched, she found that her whole body ached, oddly and not unpleasantly. There was a strange scent, not the lavender-scented linen of her pillows that she was used to.

She groaned and rolled over on to her back, opening one eye.

It was full morning, clearly, but there was not the blaze of light she expected when she woke up. Coming fully awake, she opened both eyes and sat up, looking about her in dismay. The events of last night returned with a rush all too vividly. Oh God, what had she done?

She was alone. It was clear from the tangled afghan, and even more from the rough cushions that had served as a pillow, that she had not slept alone. She flushed. The afghan had fallen as she sat up, and she realised with another start of memory that she was naked. She gathered the rough wool to her breast, flushing harder.

There were sounds beyond the cabin. She might have woken alone, but it was clear that Ruy had not left the boat. Panic took hold of her, then her throat closed as the wooden door swung open.

He stood there, looking behind him. He was wearing last night's slinky trousers and nothing else. There were drops of water on his hair, and his bare chest gleamed in the sunlight pouring through the tiny porthole. Barbara felt her nerves curl into a deep contraction of longing at the sight, and could have died with shame. By the time he turned his head, she had a hold on herself.

She met his eyes wryly. 'I see you've got rid of that ridiculous tail,' she said in a careless tone she was rather proud of.

Ruy looked startled. Then his smile broke out and he sat on the end of the bunk.

'It fell victim to one of the musketeers last night. He took it as a trophy for opening a bottle of champagne faster than I could,' he told her.

He was, thought Barbara, disgustingly cheerful. It could not have been more obvious that this was not the first time he had woken up after a party in

the arms of a dishevelled lady. He looked relaxed
and offensively pleased with himself.

'What's the time?' she asked abruptly.

His eyebrows flew up. 'Why?'

'We have guests,' she reminded him.

He chuckled. 'They'll all be in bed and asleep.'
He grinned at her. 'They didn't have the benefit of
the early night that we had.'

How dared he sit there laughing at her? How
dared he? Barbara came close to hating him, feeling
the blood scorch her skin. The fact that he in-
spected her blush interestedly did not make her feel
any more charitably inclined towards him.

'You look as if you're suffering from a bad case
of morning-after conscience,' said Ruy, amused.
He flicked the end of her nose with a long finger.
'Don't worry—in our case, it's legal.'

She looked away, willing her blush to die down.
Her fingers were clenched into the afghan like
claws.

'What *is* the time?'

He looked at her and then, shrugging, went to
the porthole and lowered his head to peer out. The
sun caught his hair and turned it blue-black.
Barbara wanted to touch it so much that it hurt.
She shut her eyes.

'About eight, I imagine. Lots of time.'

She opened her eyes quickly. 'Time for what?'

He advanced on her, his bare feet soundless on
the oak boards. 'Guess.'

She hugged the afghan to her and jumped back
against the bulkhead. 'No!'

Ruy was puzzled, but not yet put out. Oh, it was all some game to him, she thought between rage and misery. He must have done this so often, he knew to a millimetre how to touch, how to talk, how to bring the little scene back to everyday—and how to send it out into orbit again. Well, she was not taking off again, not in the cold light of day when she knew that she loved him and that he did not love her. Last night she had been reckless. This morning she was counting the cost.

'If you were thinking of taking people early morning tea in your English fashion, I can assure you no one will thank you,' he said, reaching for her. His mouth travelled softly along her hairline. Barbara breathed carefully and did not allow her screaming muscles to relent.

Ruy leaned back, his eyes watchful. 'What's wrong?'

She shook her head. 'What should be wrong?'

Just for a moment he looked disturbed. 'You tell me.'

'You're imagining it,' she said with a forced laugh.

His brows twitched together in a hard line. 'Am I?'

In one of his lightning movements, he pulled the rug away from her. She grabbed it too late, her hands fell, and she looked at him with undisguised distress. For a moment they stared at each other without speaking.

Then, slowly, he gave her the wool covering back. She seized it thankfully, huddling it around her, stammering some stuff about it being cold in the boat. It was untrue and they both knew it. He turned away. Without a word, he left the cabin.

At once Barbara scrambled off the bunk. She knew without having to be told that he would not come back until she emerged. She rooted among the tangle of garments on the deckboards for her own clothes. In the morning light they looked absurdly fragile, as if she had been wearing no more than the cobweb the dress professed to be.

She pulled the silky tights and the lacy underwear on as if they were regulation orphanage issue. In the morning light the dress looked almost transparent: Barbara blenched. How had it looked last night under the glare of those party lights? How had she looked? As if she wanted to be carried off to some secluded corner? Flappers had nurtured the reputation for mild wickedness, hadn't they? She had not thought of that before, but perhaps Ruy had. Perhaps, seeing her in this wispy dress, with its provocatively modest air and glimpses of flesh as the material wafted, he had thought she wanted, for once, to be a little daring.

Barbara closed her eyes and leaned her aching forehead against the bulkhead. It was her own fault, after all. She had known last night, when she had thrown caution to the winds, that there would be a price for taking what she wanted.

There was only one thing for it. She would have to go out there and behave as if it had meant no more than a passing fling, as if she were the flapper of his imagination.

He was standing at the railing, looking out down the creek towards the open sea. He looked grim.

He said, 'I found your shoes.' He nodded towards the strappy sandals, neatly set side by side at the top of the plank.

Barbara made no move towards them, and nor did he. They must, she realised, have fallen off when he'd picked her up last night. The very hint of the memory of his arms swinging her high sent a stab to her heart, and she flinched away from the picture, from the remembered closeness.

'I won't put them on until I've negotiated the bank,' she said in a high false voice.

Ruy nodded. 'I won't offer to carry you.'

The tide was lower now, the plank not at such a suicidal angle. Barbara got across it somehow, conscious all the time of his eyes on her and the murky water on either side of the plank.

When she was safely on shore he followed her lithely, his bare feet very sure. 'Well, then,' he said lightly, 'breakfast.'

And he maintained an exchange of intimidating sophistication all the way back to the house.

They ate a substantial breakfast, sitting at the kitchen table while Elena cheerfully scrambled them eggs and heated rolls. Unlike Barbara, she was quite undismayed by Ruy's bare-chested, unshaven state. But then she presumably did not want to fling herself against that chest or rub her face against that brigand's chin.

For Barbara, the meal was a nightmare. Her constraint grew by the minute. In the end she could barely keep still, and she was answering their cheery remarks with monosyllables. At last she could bear it no more. 'I'm stiff. I could do with a bath,' she murmured, getting to her feet.

Ruy gave a nasty crack of laughter which Elena ignored. Or maybe it did not sound nasty to her. Barbara gave him a smile aimed somewhere in the direction of his right ear, and retreated.

Ruy was right, most of their other guests were still in bed. They did not really begin to drift downstairs again until early afternoon. Elena kept a running buffet in the kitchen from which they picked in a desultory way. And in the evening they had a barbecue on the beach.

Barbara managed to submerge herself in hostessing and avoid Ruy. Not that he seemed to be seeking her out.

Dick, however, was a different matter. He came and sat beside her on the beach that evening. She was turning sausages and steaks on the large barbecue they had brought down to the shore. Ruy was opening bottles while Pedro circulated with glasses.

'It's good to see you,' said Dick. 'Both of you. I never thought Ruy would do it, you know.'

Barbara winced, and turned over a flaring piece of meat.

'Do what? Marry? Or, marry me?'

He stared. 'Why, marry you, of course. We thought he was fixed up with Pepita. We knew he had to marry after Fernando died.'

So even Dick knew that Pepita was Ruy's first love! Well, the engagement had been no secret, and there was no reason for Ruy to have kept his feelings secret either. Nor had she ever thought anything else. Why did it hurt so much, then? The faint ache she had felt all day in her body became a pain.

'It's terrific to see him so happy,' Dick went on, oblivious.

'I suppose you never thought he could be happy either?' Barbara asked waspishly.

'No,' he agreed, too ingenuous to see her annoyance, and at once she was ashamed of herself. He picked up a sausage and began to chew it. 'He's had a lot of bad luck.' He shuffled and then said in an embarrassed voice, 'Sort of made him suspicious, not being able to trust—er—people he—er—ought to be able to trust. If you know what I mean.'

Pepita again, she thought.

'I know what you mean,' Barbara said in a stifled voice.

Dick beamed at her. 'Good. So it's great to see he's stopped...'

He broke off as another guest came up looking for food which Barbara supplied.

Stopped what? she thought. Chasing rainbows? By putting Pepita out of his mind and making do with his wife? Somehow the thought that Ruy was making do with his wife was the most unendurable of all.

They did not really have time to talk for the next three days. First of all their guests lingered, then

Barbara flung herself into the cleaning up operation. But, although they were civilised and friendly, that thought festered. It became an obsession. Even while she was Hoovering the Chinese rugs, or polishing parquet flooring—to which Elena objected volubly—Barbara could not put it out of her head. And, when she retired to her lonely room as late as she dared, it came to mock her like an unfriendly ghost.

In the end, it was Ruy who forced a confrontation.

She came down in the morning to find that he was already out. Elena announced that he had ridden over to Pepita's, leaving a message that if Barbara was up early enough she should follow him and they would ride back along the shore. Barbara set her teeth and thanked Elena for the message. She ignored the early hour on the kitchen clock and set to work polishing mirrors in the main salon.

She worked ferociously all morning until she heard doors, voices, and the double doors behind her were flung open.

Ruy came in without speaking. He looked a little tired and dusty, and his face was set. He had an air of resolution that filled Barbara with foreboding, as he carefully shut the doors behind him.

'Barbara, we have to talk,' he said quietly.

She clutched her duster to her breast, aware of the incongruity and unable to begin to laugh at it. Had he seen Pepita and decided that it was hopeless; that he must be with the woman he loved or with no one? Or—worse—that he would make the best of his second-rate bargain? She bent her shining head, and did not see how his mouth tightened. For a moment he looked anguished.

She bit her lip. 'Why?'

He made an impatient gesture. 'You must see things have changed.'

Since he had seen Pepita again. Since he had treated his wife like one of his sophisticated companions and taken her to bed on the crest of wine and music.

Barbara said desperately, 'I don't want anything to change.'

There was a little silence.

Then Ruy said, 'I'm afraid it's too late for that.' He was very gentle.

Tears flooded her eyes. 'Please,' she said under her breath, imploring.

She could hardly see him, her eyes were swimming so, but it seemed to her that he looked grim.

'My dear...don't look like that!' It sounded torn out of him.

She swallowed and tried valiantly to master her voice. 'I'm sorry. I'm trying to be sensible.'

Sensible while he told her that his heart was irrevocably Pepita's? *Sensible?* She felt like tearing the walls of the house down, screaming her hurt out to the world. But it was her own fault. She had asked for it and she must bear it.

Ruy echoed her own thoughts. 'Being sensible doesn't seem to be relevant, somehow. It hasn't done me much good, anyway.'

She began, 'What...' but broke off when she saw his face. He looked like a man facing a battle he knew would be his last.

'I can't go on,' he said simply. 'Not like this.'

She made a small sound, not much of one, like an animal startled by pain. He whitened. She could see that he meant it. She had never seen him more serious. Seeing Pepita again must have been a revelation, she thought viciously, anger beginning to stir.

'Why did you marry me, Ruy?' she asked in despair.

His head went up as if she had hit him. To her surprise, he seemed lost for an answer. Could he not face spelling out the harsh truth about their cold-blooded arrangement, though they both knew it perfectly well?

'Why?' she insisted, giving him no quarter.

He said on a note of horrified discovery, 'I've hurt you.'

Her laugh gave him the truth better than any words.

'Why?' she asked again.

He passed a weary hand over his eyes. 'It was a gamble, a risk. I had to *try*... Can't you see that? I never meant to hurt you.'

But she was beyond being fair. 'What did you think would happen? Did you think I wouldn't find out?'

Under the tan, Ruy was very pale. He said quietly, 'It must seem ridiculous to you, but I thought I could control it.'

Barbara cried out as if she had been shot. He started towards her, but stopped as she flinched. His hand went to his marred cheek and he closed his eyes.

'I'm more sorry than I can say. I hoped...'

Hoped that he would forget Pepita? Barbara made a choked sound, half laugh, half protest.

He did come to her side then, swiftly. She flung up a hand to stop him, twisting away from that powerful body. Ruy stopped at once, his scar pulsing savagely.

'What do you want me to do?' Ruy asked at last. He sounded infinitely weary.

Love me, thought Barbara. She almost said it. It seemed her powers of self-control were rapidly leaving her. The only thing for it was to get out before she terminally embarrassed both of them.

'Let me go,' she said, half to herself.

She saw his throat move. Then, very deliberately, he stood back against the wall, his hands spread palm outward, empty. The way was open. She pushed past him before the tears, finally and humiliatingly, spilled over.

If she had not been half blinded by tears, she would not have made for the little creek. There were too many memories there, too many memories on the shore where they had taken their morning rides. But she was desperate and went where her feet took her.

Eventually she found herself on the beach, labouring to walk on the powdery dunes among the sea stock and spiky grasses. She tried to take hold of her whirling thoughts. She must go back, of course, find what he wanted to do, be civilised.

She was so deeply immersed that she did not see the figure coming towards her. He had put a hand on her shoulder before she raised her head. 'Oh, lord,' she said. Somehow it was inevitable that Harry would turn up now.

Characteristically, his first words were a reproach. 'I've been waiting around for days. I thought you'd come sooner.'

Barbara looked at him wearily.

'I gave that spoilt kid a message.'

'Luis?' She was bewildered. 'You gave Luis a message for me? Why?'

Harry made a significant movement, rubbing his first fingers and thumb together. When Barbara stared uncomprehending he gave a wink and said, 'Money.'

She could have laughed. 'I told you, Harry—no more.'

He ignored it. 'Want me to talk to him at the big house, do you?' He gave one of his boisterous laughs to show he did not—quite—mean the threat.

Barbara began to realise that she did not like her Uncle Harry very much. 'No,' she said decisively.

He pulled her back viciously. 'Do you want it all for yourself, then? He must be the wealthiest man on the coast.'

The scene in the salon had left her with no feelings left on minor matters, she found. She shook him off.

'Harry, you're a crook and a conman. You've spoiled my life for years with your demands and your tales of my father. I don't care for myself any more, but you're not going to do it to the man I love.'

'You're a fool,' he said, staring at her as if he did not believe his ears.

Barbara's smile was wry. Her uncle would not appreciate the truth of his words. 'Undoubtedly,' she said, turning away.

This time Harry did more than turn her round; he slapped her hard, as he had when she had been a recalcitrant teenager. She staggered, her feet losing purchase in the sand. Too late, she saw that he was beside himself. She began to be afraid. The disappointment of his hopes had pushed him into fury. Barbara put up her arms to try to save herself, but she was off balance and Harry was fired with his sense of outrage. He hit her again and again. She had no breath to cry out, trying to hold him off, scrabbling with her feet in the sand to try to run.

And then, suddenly, it was over: Harry was plucked off her as if he were nothing more than a troublesome leaf that had blown about her legs. She heard the thud as he hit the sand beyond her. Sobbing, scrubbing at her eyes, Barbara tried to straighten.

For the third time in her life she was lifted and held against a muscular chest. Ruy's breathing was not even ruffled. He turned his back on Harry without a word. She said his name in wonder, her voice breaking. He looked down at her, and she began to tremble.

'Ruy, you can't...' She had been going to say that he could not carry her all the way up to the house, but he stopped her, his eyes amused, and behind the amusement there was a blaze of tenderness that dazzled her.

'My darling Barbara, that is something you are never going to say to me again,' he told her superbly.

And she was silenced.

CHAPTER TEN

HE TOOK her to her own room.

'Oh no! Oh, really, I'm not ill,' Barbara protested shyly.

Ruy grinned down at her. 'You've had a shock. Or if you haven't, I have.'

She considered him. 'Are we going to my room for your benefit or mine?'

'Both,' he said promptly, laughing down at her.

He shouldered open the door and went inside. Elena had not yet cleared last night's coffee-tray from the rosewood table, though the room was otherwise tidy. Barbara had been convulsively tidying it for days, once she had made the bed, which did not take nearly long enough.

Ruy strode over to the bed and dropped her on it gently. He stood for a moment looking anxiously down into her face.

'How do you feel?'

Barbara shook her head. 'Like a fraud. There's no need for all this tender loving care—really.'

'There is every need,' Ruy said calmly, dropping down beside her and taking her in his arms.

Barbara did not even attempt to resist. She gave herself up to his kiss as if she had never heard of self-preservation. At last he lifted his head and gave a long sigh that was more than half a groan.

'I told you—I needed that. I thought you were never going to let me near you again.'

She laid her hand against the side of his face, marvelling. Then, suddenly what he said registered, and she angled her head to look at him.

'What do you mean?'

'You were going away,' he pointed out, his arms tightening.

'But——' Barbara broke off, trying to make sense of the warmth in his face and the unmistakable passion in his hold.

'But . . .?' he prompted, watching her carefully.

She flushed. 'That was because you didn't need me,' she said on a rush of honesty.

There was a silence. She could not look at him, but his arms did not relax.

At last Ruy said thoughtfully. 'So that's it.' He rolled away and propped himself on one elbow, looking down at her. 'Whenever did I not need you?' he demanded, amused.

Barbara closed her eyes against the seduction of his laughter. 'You wanted a wife. You *needed* Pepita. I just happened to come along conveniently when you couldn't have her.'

He gave a great shout of laughter. 'My darling girl, if there's one thing you aren't, it's convenient. I've spent more time on you than any other woman in my whole life.' He sobered. 'Ten years of it,' he added quietly.

Her eyes flew open. *'What?'*

'Ten years,' he repeated obligingly, his mouth quirking.

'I don't believe you,' said Barbara from the heart. And, when he did not answer, she went on, groping with her memories. 'You despised me. You called me a blackmailer.'

His mouth tightened like a vice. But when he spoke his voice was calm enough. 'Oh yes, my fiendish temper. I didn't really think you were a blackmailer. Of course I didn't.'

Barbara swallowed. 'You paid me to go away,' she reminded him.

It was his turn to stare. 'What are you talking about?'

'You asked me if it was enough,' she said, wincing at the memory.

Ruy went white. 'Oh, God!'

'Don't you remember?' she challenged him.

'Oh yes, I remember.' His voice was grim. 'I remember every word I ever said to you. And most of those I didn't, God help me. How could you be such a fool? How could I, for that matter?' He drew a long breath. 'I didn't pay you to go. I didn't *want* you to go, for my sins. But everyone kept telling me it wasn't fair... And you said you wanted to go back to England... And your uncle was clearly a nasty customer and you ought to have your chance... I gave you the money to get you home. Nothing else.'

She remembered the intensity in his eyes, the strange tension in him as he'd thrust the money at her.

'Nothing else? Honestly?'

'No,' he admitted. He hesitated. 'There was something else—I don't know if you can understand.'

Barbara struggled up on her elbows. There was something here which she had to understand. It was very important. It was perhaps the most important thing in her existence. With painful intensity she searched his face, seeing the green eyes, forest-dark and watchful; the agonising slash of the scar across his cheek that betrayed him whenever he was tense; the sensual, vulnerable mouth.

'Tell me,' she whispered at last. 'Please, my love.'

He caught her hand and took it to his face, cradling his cheek in it with sudden passion. The swift, clumsy little gesture took her breath away. His fingers were shaking.

'I was—giving you a chance.'

'A chance?' she echoed, bewildered.

'To get away. From the unhappy memories. From your uncle.' He swallowed. 'From me.'

Barbara said disbelievingly, 'You sent me away! You didn't want me.'

Ruy turned his lips into the palm of her hand and the delicate touch made her shiver somewhere in the deepest centre of her blood.

'Didn't I?'

'But——'

He looked up at her. Suddenly his eyes were molten, emerald fire, no longer veiled and unreadable, but naked with feeling.

'I wanted you the moment I saw you. More than that.'

Her pulses began to slam.

'You were so lovely,' said Ruy softly. 'So alive. I'd forgotten people could look like that: just happy with the joy of living. You used to laugh with Pepita. With those children riding on the beach with you. I used to watch you like a lovesick adolescent.'

Barbara made some sound and his smile slipped into wryness.

'I—never guessed,' she said at last, unevenly.

Ruy shook his dark head. 'I took good care that you shouldn't. You were still a child. It was unforgivable of me.'

Barbara said with concentration, 'I was eighteen. That's over the age of consent, even in Portugal.'

He frowned. 'That's not what I meant. You were still innocent.'

'If you mean I was a backward adolescent, say so,' she told him stringently.

Ruy looked startled, then he laughed. 'It isn't what I mean, exactly. I didn't want to force you to grow up faster than you would naturally, that's all.'

Her eyes narrowed. 'I don't follow you.'

He sank down and pulled her round to look at him.

'Barbara, my love, I was in love with you. You were—young for your age. I was thirty. What was I supposed to do? The more I saw you, the more I wanted—more than I could have. It imposed constraints.' He let her go, rolling over on to his back, one arm thrown over his eyes. 'That's why I lost my temper with you that day, I suppose. I'd been riding myself on a very tight rein for too long, wanting the impossible.'

Suddenly, vividly, Barbara recalled Elena's oddly admonitoiry tone when she had reminded him that day that Barbara was still very young. It began to fall into place. With her outgrown clothes and her fall of ponyish hair, she must have looked a child quite a lot of the time. With Elena warning him, and probably the Marquesa too, and his own sense of the difference between their ages...

'It was another of those gambles of yours,' she said on a note of discovery. 'When you gave me the money, I mean. To see whether I'd run away or not. And if I did—well, that solved your problem. What if I hadn't?' she flung at him, suddenly bright-eyed.

He did not move the masking arm from his eyes. 'I'm not a saint. Sooner or later I'd have tried to make love to you.'

Barbara pondered it, then she asked softly, 'As you did in England? Before you asked me to marry you?'

Ruy's whole body tensed. He did not answer. Barbara began to feel as if a great weight were lifting from her.

'You know,' she said, carefully casual, 'I thought you asked me to sleep with you because you really didn't care, one way or the other.'

That brought the shielding arm away from his face.

'Pepita,' she explained in a neutral tone, 'said that you wouldn't ask a woman you wanted to make your wife—a woman you respected—to be your lover.'

'Did she?' Ruy said drily. 'When was that?'

'When she was begging me to return your ring. She was worried about that side of things, I think,' Barbara admitted, flushing faintly.

'Yes.' His face was sombre. 'Poor Pepita, I didn't treat her very well, and she's a good friend. I thought it would work. In the beginning I was so desperate about Felicia and Luis, and Pepita was just across the bay, she seemed the ideal answer. But it was crazy, of course, and she knew it before I did. Pepita knows me very well.'

'So she was right? Then why did you ask me to spend the night with you?'

Ruy almost glared at her. 'Yes, she was right. It's against all my principles. But you—God help me, you make me break all the rules, including my own.' He pulled himself up so that his face was on a level with her own. 'Did you think I ever intended to lay a hand on you ten years ago? I was supposed to be the chivalrous knight who rescued you from your uncle and that appalling business associate of his and asked nothing for himself, and what did I do? I flung myself on you like a sex-mad schoolboy.' He sounded disgusted. 'You've probably forgotten, but I haven't. I've never regretted anything more in my life.'

Barbara flinched. But now was not the time to be hiding real feelings.

She said quietly, 'I never forgot for a single day.'

His chin went up as if she had stabbed him. She wanted to touch him, but she was not quite brave enough for that. Instead her hands twisted together. She swallowed.

'There's never been anyone else, Ruy. Not even on the furthest horizon. I—thought it was because you'd hurt me.'

He closed his eyes. Barbara could not bear the look of hurt on his face. She took her courage in both hands.

'I didn't realise it was love, you see. Not until we married.'

Ruy's eyes flew open, sought hers, locked.

'Love?' he said in a cracked whisper.

Barbara nodded gravely. 'Every time anyone touched me—or tried to touch me—I'd remember that last day, in your study, when you—held me. And I couldn't bear it.'

'Oh, my darling,' he said. 'It was only a kiss. It shouldn't have frightened you so badly. It shows how young you were, after all. They were all quite right, you see.'

'I wasn't,' Barbara said fiercely, 'frightened. Not then and not now. I wanted you Ruy. What hurt was when I thought you didn't want me. Now——' She could not bring herself to look him in the face, but out of the corner of her eye she could see his scar clench and the muscle below his eye leap madly. It gave her hope. 'Now, I think I may have been wrong.' She paused. 'Will you answer me something honestly, Ruy?'

He looked at her downbent head. 'Yes,' he said simply.

'Are you in love with Pepita?'

'No,' he said. It was more convincing than any elaborate protestations.

Hugely relieved, her eyes flew to his. In pure reflex, their hands reached out and clasped.

'Pepita is a friend,' Ruy said again. 'You are my love.'

Barbara wanted to believe him, but she had been too insecure for too long. 'One day—you might not remember—we were talking about what we wanted if we could have anything—you said you'd had what you wanted once.' She looked down at their clasped hands. 'If you meant Pepita, being engaged to her, I can take it. Please don't lie to me, Ruy, not even to make me happy,' she finished in a low voice.

His fingers tightened painfully. 'I meant you,' he said starkly. 'Eighteen years old and the love of my life. I told you I didn't deserve it, either—do you remember that? Well, I meant it. I felt I was no better than that man who attacked you. I'll never forget finding you in the orchard as long as I live. And then I—blew my cool and tried to make love to you. My darling, you should have seen yourself— pale and shocked, and desperate to get away.'

Barbara realised that the ten-year-old encounter had been as big a nightmare for Ruy as it had been for her. She returned the pressure of his fingers. 'Only because you'd called me a blackmailer. And,' she swallowed, 'I was ashamed.'

He said remorsefully, 'That was my fault. I knew you'd never have anything to do with your Uncle Harry's schemes...'

But she stopped him. 'No. Not of Harry and my family. I was ashamed of myself. Me. The way I— was with you. You probably don't remember, but...'

'Remember?' he interrupted fiercely. 'Dear God, there hasn't been a day since then I haven't remembered and wondered.' He looked at her, his eyes very clear. 'If I hadn't stopped—and I very nearly didn't—would it have made any difference? I've never made love to a virgin...' He stopped as Barbara began to chuckle, his eyes narrowed.

'Oh yes, you have,' she said, suddenly amazingly happy.

Ruy said hoarsely, 'But I thought...'

'You thought I'd have had the good sense to forget you?' Barbara murmured, reaching up to him, her mouth curving. 'Mm, you would, wouldn't you? But I told you, Ruy, there's been no one else. I was pretty blank ten years ago, but at least I knew that I didn't want anyone else.'

He held her away from him. 'But you were going to leave me,' he said, his mouth a thin line as he searched her face. 'Today, this morning, you were distressed. You were going away.'

'Because I thought it was still Pepita you wanted!' she shouted at him, punching her fist against the wall of his chest. 'You kept saying you couldn't control it, and I thought you wanted her back.'

Ruy was incredulous. 'But my darling Barbara, it was you I'd made mad passionate love to,' he said in exasperation. 'There's only one woman who fuses my control.'

She stared. 'Then why did you say you couldn't go on?'

He bent her back among the pillows, baring his teeth at her.

'Because I couldn't. I was going mad keeping my hands off you, but it seemed to be what you wanted. Why the hell did you do that to me, to both of us, if it wasn't?'

Barbara was dazed. 'Because I didn't want to embarrass you,' she said with absolute sincerity.

'Embarrass...?' He flexed his fingers round her throat. 'I could murder you,' he said conversationally. 'Embarrass me, for God's sake?'

'I cared so much,' muttered Barbara, feeling her face grow hot.

Ruy raised his head and gave a howl. 'And I didn't? When you walked into my house that day in London and nothing had changed in ten years and I had to have you?'

Her fingers trembled against the warmth of his chest.

'You mean then? At once? The first day?' asked Barbara, shaken.

'The first minute,' he told her.

'But...'

He stopped her. 'I rang Pepita the moment you'd gone. She was waiting for me.'

'What?'

Ruy gave her a rueful grin. 'Pepita,' he said with deliberation, 'was playing Cupid. We'd been talking of you the previous evening—I'd found out where you worked—and something seemed to have roused her suspicions. She was having second thoughts about marrying me anyway, I suspect. Anyway, she thought from something I said or didn't say that I must have had more of an interest in you ten years ago than she had thought. And she was fairly sure that you had had—as she put it—a crush on me.'

Barbara gave a strangled protest.

'I must say,' a smile curled his mouth, 'I found that rather encouraging. At the time, I hadn't noticed anything. But just then I was still bruised—I wasn't used to being a gargoyle and I didn't think anyone could look at me without feeling sick, least of all a gorgeous English girl who...'

'Didn't wear enough clothes,' Barbara supplied wryly, remembering Pepita's strictures from all those years before.

Ruy laughed. 'They were maybe a bit skimpy,' he allowed. 'It was a disappointment to find you'd gone into business suits and high-necked blouses, I confess.'

'You said I hadn't changed,' she reminded him accusingly.

'I hoped you hadn't. And——' he hesitated, '—it felt as if you hadn't. As if whatever it was between us was still there, needing to be dealt with.'

'So you tried to seduce me?' Barbara said, remembering the night of the riverside hotel when she had so nearly fallen victim to his charm. If only she had!

'I got a bit carried away,' Ruy admitted.

'You chanced your arm,' Barbara corrected. She ran her hands flat over the smooth skin of his torso, and he shivered with pleasure.

'And nearly lost you for my pains.'

She shook her head. 'I don't think so.'

'You gave a good imitation, then,' he said drily. 'I thought after that I'd burnt my boats, that's why I came to you pleading about Luis and Felicia. What I wanted to say was that I loved you madly and my life was incomplete without you. But it seemed too big a thing to lay on you—after just a few days like that—and I hadn't exactly behaved like Sir Galahad, either. So I tried to be subtle, and put us both into hell.'

'Machiavelli,' she murmured. 'I hope Luis hasn't taken your lessons too closely to heart.'

He began to laugh very softly.

'I was so brilliant a strategist, I nearly lost you. I'd faced that. It was only when I heard you say to the awful Harry "the man I love" that I had any idea that I might have any hope left.' He was suddenly not smiling any more, his whole body tense as he looked down at her, his green eyes utterly without pretence. 'I couldn't believe it. Even now... Was I wrong, Barbara? Will you give me another chance?'

She looked at him lovingly. Very carefully, she cupped his face with both hands, moulding her fingers over the marred cheek and the smooth one alike.

'The man I love doesn't need another chance,' she said softly.

Ruy drew in a long breath. And then he made love to her as if he had never made love before, with infinite care, in a slow, gentle exploration of their bodies' responses. In the end it was Barbara who writhed, sobbing, reaching for heaven, and making Ruy loose the last constricting restraint he had placed upon himself and his love for her.

Afterwards they slept a little, awoke to golden sunshine, laughed and made love again in a blaze of serene and mutual passion. Miraculously, they were undisturbed, as—a long time later—Barbara observed drowsily.

'No miracle, my darling,' murmured Ruy, the thread of amusement which she would always recognise in his voice. 'I told Elena as soon as we arrived that whenever we were up here together she should busy herself downstairs and leave us alone until we came down. I had been thinking it was an unnecessary precaution,' he added ruefully. He tickled her nose. 'I'm glad it wasn't.'

'You're a practised seducer,' Barbara said without rancour. She caught the mischievous fingers and kissed them. 'I forgive you.'

'Well, thank God for that, at least!'

'But it was a miracle that you came down to the beach when I was with Harry,' she said, waking up a little. 'That was amazingly lucky.'

'No, it wasn't. It was Luis,' Ruy said matter-of-factly.

She stared.

'Apparently Harry'd been hanging around there for days, trying to get Luis to fetch you. When he saw him—and you—this morning, he decided that he didn't like it and came to get me. There may,' added Ruy thoughtfully, 'be more to that child than I thought.'

Barbara swallowed. 'Did he know it was my uncle?'

'No. He thought he was some sort of tramp.' Ruy hugged her against him. 'He was afraid he would hurt you.'

She shivered. 'Did you—realise?'

He turned his head and kissed her eyebrow. 'I guessed. I'd been expecting him to turn up at some point.'

She looked up swiftly into his face, surprised by his casual tone. 'Don't you care?'

'Care?' He looked down at her, frowning. 'I care that he hurt you, very much. If he turns up again, I shall have great pleasure in throwing him down the steps, aged uncle or no. But not otherwise.'

Barbara bit her lip. 'He's a rogue, though.'

'Certainly,' Ruy sounded puzzled.

'And he's my relative. I mean, it's in the blood,' she said, not very clearly but with great shame in her voice.

Ruy's puzzlement evaporated. He settled a long arm more comfortably round her shoulderblades and rubbed his chin over and over her as if he were soothing a child.

'We all have ghastly relatives. It's one of the hazards of being born,' he said drily. 'My own brother was a pretty fine specimen, I'm afraid.'

She spread her hands over his chest, sensing the suppressed feeling.

He went on quietly, 'You may know that he was responsible for my scar. Most people think it was an accident. It wasn't. He was in a blind temper and he came for me with his fishing knife.'

Barbara made a little sound of distress, pressing closer, murmuring.

'It's all right, I'm over it now.' Ruy gave a soft laugh. 'It gave me a bad moment when I thought *you* couldn't bear the sight of me because of my face, but I soon got over that. You were always honest, and it didn't seem to me that you minded.' His voice was calm, but Barbara heard the uncertainty.

She pulled up on to one elbow and looked down very openly into his eyes.

'I love everything about you,' she told him. She kissed the scarred tissue below his eye. 'Including that.' She felt with satisfaction the increase of his heartbeat against her skin. 'You've convinced me,' she murmured. 'You overlook Harry, I'll forget about your brother, or vice versa.'

Beneath her moulding fingers, Ruy's chest heaved. He was, she realised, laughing, a deep, pleased chuckle that was full of delighted surprise.

'Right,' he agreed. 'Whatever you say. Is that your last problem before we settle down to marital bliss? Or have you any neuroses tucked away there?'

She waved her clenched fist in the direction of his chin.

'Who was responsible for my neuroses?' she said indignantly. 'Who was so haughty, and distant and...and unfeeling, that I tied myself up in knots?'

'Guilty,' said Ruy, catching her hand and unfolding the fingers so he could kiss each one. 'Guilty and humbly repentant. Let me make reparation.'

Barbara looked at him suspiciously. He did not sound repentant.

'How?'

He ran a long finger along her lower lip, and chuckled softly as her breath caught and her eyes went dark.

'By helping you undo the knots?' he suggested helpfully.

He slid his other hand the length of her thigh. Her blood began to beat in uneven tempo. Indignant, she tried to move away, but he would not let her.

'They're my knots too,' he whispered. 'Help me.' He kissed her lingeringly. 'I told you, once, I'd give you anything I could. Let me.'

So Barbara did, in the end, ask him for what she wanted, secure in the absolute trust that she already had it and it was mutual.

She held his head steady for her slow kiss.

'Love me,' she said.

Harlequin Presents

Coming Next Month

Available in March wherever paperback books are sold, or through
Harlequin Reader Service:

In the U.S.
901 Fuhrmann Blvd.
P.O. Box 1397
Buffalo, N.Y. 14240-1397

In Canada
P.O. Box 603
Fort Erie, Ontario
L2A 5X3

February brings you...

Harlequin Presents...

PENNY JORDAN

valentine's night

Sorrel didn't particularly want to meet her long-lost cousin Val from Australia. However, since the girl had come all this way just to make contact, it seemed a little churlish not to welcome her.

As there was no room at home, it was agreed that Sorrel and Val would share the Welsh farmhouse that was being renovated for Sorrel's brother and his wife. Conditions were a bit primitive, but that didn't matter.

At least, not until Sorrel found herself snowed in with the long-lost cousin, who turned out to be a handsome, six-foot male!

Also, look for the next Harlequin Presents Award of Excellence title in April:

Elusive as the Unicorn
by Carole Mortimer

HP1243-1

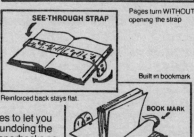

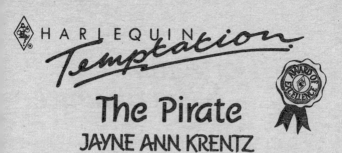

The Pirate
JAYNE ANN KRENTZ

At the heart of every powerful romance story lies a
legend. There are many romantic legends and
countless modern variations on them, but they all
have one thing in common: They are tales of brave,
resourceful women who must gentle and tame the
powerful, passionate men who are their true mates.

The enormous appeal of Jayne Ann Krentz lies in
her ability to create modern-day versions of these
classic romantic myths, and her LADIES AND
LEGENDS trilogy showcases this talent. Believing
that a storyteller who can bring legends to life
deserves special attention, Harlequin has chosen
the first book of the trilogy—THE PIRATE—to
receive our Award of Excellence. Look for it now.

AE-PIR-1A

Harlequin Superromance®

LET THE GOOD TIMES ROLL...

Add some Cajun spice to liven up your New Year's
celebrations and join Superromance for a romantic
tour of the rich Acadian marshlands and the legendary
Louisiana bayous.

Starting in January 1990, we're launching CAJUN
MELODIES, a three-book tribute to the fun-loving
people who've enriched America by introducing us to
crawfish étouffé and gumbo, zydeco music and the
Saturday night party, the *fais-dodo*. And learn about
loving, Cajun-style, as you meet the tall, dark,
handsome men who win their ladies' hearts with a
beautiful, haunting melody....

Book One: *Julianne's Song*, January 1990
Book Two: *Catherine's Song*, February 1990
Book Three: *Jessica's Song*, March 1990

SRCJ-1R